Jeannie —
True Love never dies!
xoxo

Rebuild My Love

REBUILD MY LOVE

Lisa Carlson

ISBN-13: 978-1511618304
ISBN-10: 1511618302

NICK

Fuck. My. Life.

It's Monday morning and I'm three fucking guys short. Max is on his honeymoon which means I can't really be pissed off at him, but Jesse and Alex got drunk at some BBQ yesterday and were too hung over to come in today. To top it all off, the *Dragon Lady* was gracing us with one of her daily "visits" to the jobsite.

"Nick, I think this window is on the wrong side of the room. Shouldn't it be over there," she calls over her shoulder at me and points her perfectly manicured finger at an interior wall. *Seriously?*

It takes every ounce of self-control not to snatch the plans out of her hands and tell her to fuck off. My fingers itch to bury my claw hammer between her sculpted eyebrows.

I sigh. "Mrs. Glickman, I think you're holding the blueprints upside down again." Walking over to her, I gently reposition the plans she's holding.

She glances over the plans again. "You know, I think you may be right."

Gee thanks, lady.

She puts the plans on the kitchen countertop and heads toward the foyer. "How are we doing on the new powder room?" Looking at the new space, a scowl mars her face. "I thought the tile would be in by now."

Me too, and it would have been if Jesse and Alex showed up today. I plaster on a smile and lie through my teeth.

"I apologize, Mrs. Glickman, it seems there was an error with the tile and my crew is out now getting the new order."

"Humph. Are you sure this will all be done on time? My daughter's baby shower is in six weeks and you only have four left. I don't see much improvement on the kitchen and the powder room is basically a hole. Your father assured me this would be done on time. I'm not paying you any more money, either."

My hand moves toward the hammer on my tool belt, but I stop myself before making contact. "Yes, Mrs. Glickman, it will be done on time."

I wanted to tell her that her daily "visits" were slowing down our progress, but she was paying my dad a shitload of money so I kept my mouth shut. Personally I think she checks in to make sure we aren't stealing any of her precious knick-knacks. The woman has a strange obsession with owls and they are everywhere. It's fuckin' creepy.

Dr. Glickman is a local podiatrist who indulges his wife Harriet and daughter Sadie to no end. Case in point, the Glickman's were currently living in their guest house because the noise and dust from the job was stressing out their little rat dog, Pookie. The dog probably weighed all of seven pounds and was always dressed in an outfit that matched Mrs. Glickman. Today's outfit consisted of a canary yellow coat on the rat dog which matched Mrs. Glickman's yellow silk blouse.

It was disturbing.

Mrs. Glickman took one more look around and ran her hand over her platinum hair. One would never guess Mrs. Glickman was in her sixties, she looked like a much younger woman. She kept in shape by playing tennis and swimming—both of which were done on their expansive estate. The house was Mrs. Glickman's childhood home; her parents were beyond loaded. She inherited the house a few years ago when her father died. According to Dr. Glickman, one of their friends had recently done some updating to their home. Not being one to be outshone by someone else, Mrs. Glickman decided she wanted to upgrade the kitchen and add a powder room by the front door to avoid people "traipsing through her house as they pleased."

"Well I hope so. Pookie and I have a massage and mani-pedis scheduled for this afternoon. I'll be back in the morning to check on the powder room tile." She breezes past me in a cloud of expensive perfume through the front door and slips into the waiting town car without a backwards glance in my direction.

"Shit." I grab my cell and make a call.

"Good morning. Zacco Construction, how may I help you?"

"Gina, I need Jesse and Alex here *now*."

Her reply could have frozen an active volcano. "Well, good morning to you too, Nick. Yes, I'm fine; thanks so much for asking."

I sigh. "Look, Gina. I'm sorry, okay? The Dragon Lady just left and she has that special way of pissing me off. I need Jesse and Alex here to get started on the fucking powder room."

"Nick, they called out sick. What do you want me to do about it?"

Why is everyone pissing me off today? "Damn it, Gina. I don't know and I don't fucking care. Just get them here within the hour, damn it!" I hang up and turn my phone off. I am tired of excuses. Stalking back into the kitchen I grab the nearest sledgehammer and take out my anger on the countertop.

GINA

I stared at the phone in my hand as the dial tone greeted me. Did Nick just bark an order at me and then hang up?

Motherfucker.

I slam down the phone as Nick's father, Dominic, walks into the office. He takes one look at me and sighs. Dominic is about five foot nine inches tall and his thick black hair was recently cut short. His deep brown eyes narrow and he crosses his arms across his broad chest. "What'd he do now?"

I like Dominic. He is only in the office two days a week; the other days he spends on various jobsites. He lets me run the office the way I want and never barks orders.

I grab my purse and slam the desk drawer closed. "Mein Fuhrer has commanded I get Alex and Jesse to the jobsite in the next" –I glance at my watch– "forty minutes! I'd better go."

Dominic's brows draw together. "Why aren't they there already?"

I shrug, moving around my desk. "They called out, but don't worry, I'll get them."

Dominic gently grabs my arm. "Don't be too mad at Nick. Mrs. Glickman is a royal pain in the ass and I know she's been giving Nick a hard time."

I sigh. "I get it, Dominic. Shit rolls downhill and I'm at the freakin' bottom of it all, but there's a way to talk to a person, ya know? I mean, I'm more than just the office manager, I'm his girlfriend."

Dominic kisses my temple. "I know, kiddo, and I'm sorry. He gets his temper from his mother, but we love them anyway, right?"

I shrug out of Dominic's grasp. "There's a difference between an asino and a signore, Dominic, and right now Nick is no signore." I slam the office door and head toward my car. About half way, I stop and look around. The hairs on the back of my neck stand on end. I scan the parking lot. Everything looks normal, but I hurry to my car and lock the doors as soon as I get in.

NICK

I was signing for the Italian tile Mrs. Glickman insisted on having for the powder room—after she'd changed her mind four times—and check my watch. I called Gina almost an hour ago and Jesse and Alex are still MIA. Jesus Christ, do I have to do *everything* myself? Reaching for my phone, I stop when Alex and Jesse came stumbling through the front door, giggling like a couple teenage girls. They looked like shit and smelled like a bar after last call. Staring at me with unfocused eyes, they slightly wave in my direction.

"Hey there, boss man. How they hanging?" Jesse leans on Alex in an effort to stay upright.

"Are you fucking kidding me right now? Why are you here if you're still drunk?"

Alex shrugs, and they stumble a little. “I dunno. Gina said to ‘get in the fucking car,’ so we did. She’s kinda scary when she’s mad, boss.”

I rush past them to find Gina leaning against her car in the driveway. She held a nail file in one hand and scowls at her nails. She glances in my direction, but keeps studying her nails, an evil smirk crossing her lips.

I stalk across the driveway and stop mere inches from the car. “Gina, what the fuck?”

She crosses her arms and glares. “Is there a problem, Mr. Zacco?” Her voice drips with sarcasm.

“You know I can’t have them here like that! I’ll get freakin' sued. Why did you bring them here?”

Gina pushes off the door and plants her hands on her hips. “I was following orders, *sir*.”

“What the hell does that mean?”

She thrust her arms forward, pushing my chest. “’Get them here within the hour, damn it.’ Sound familiar? Well here they are as *ordered*.”

I scrub hand down my face and mentally count to ten. “Baby, I’m sorry, okay? I can’t have them here.” I look over my shoulder and saw the boys passed out on the front steps. “Fuck.”

She shrugs, sliding behind the wheel. “Not my problem, *boss.* Now if you’ll excuse me, I have to go to the carwash. Jesse hung his head out the back window and puked down the side of my car on the way over here and it’s starting to smell.” Her car roars to life. “I’m taking the rest of the day off too.”

“Wait.” I point over my shoulder. “What am I supposed to do with them?”

She slips on her sunglasses. “I don’t know and I don’t care, they’re your problem now.” She backs out of the driveway without sparing me a second glance. I turn around as Alex throws up on Mrs. Glickman’s roses.

Like I said before, Fuck. My. Life.

GINA

Asshole.

I almost caved when I saw Nick. He is the spitting image of his father. The way his jeans hung on his hips made my mouth water. It took all my resolve not to kiss him. I would have forgiven him barking at me. Then he opened his mouth and ruined everything.

I turn up the music and shake my head. My car is clean, but my anger hadn't gone away. Wanting someone to commiserate with, I stop at my Uncle Ray's pizzeria to see my friend Marco.

Marco is my cousin Abby's sous chef at *Mio Angelo's*. Our Uncle Ray expanded the pizzeria to add the restaurant for Abby after she came back from cooking school in Tuscany. She and Max are in Italy on their honeymoon so Marco is running the restaurant. My mom's been helping Marco a few days a week and so far everything's gone smoothly.

A small stab of jealousy hits when thinking about Max and Abby. Don't get me wrong, I'm thrilled for them, but they married within a year of meeting each other. Max works on Nick's crew, not that he has to; apparently he's loaded, but likes to work. He and Abby met when the new restaurant was being built. They fell in love and we all thought she was crazy to get married so quickly but she just smiled and said, "When you know, you know, so why wait?"

I sigh. Nick and I have been dating for almost three years. We discussed marriage, but there's still no ring on my finger. Maybe that's my fault. You know, 'Why buy the cow if you're getting the milk for free?'

I park the car in my usual spot behind the pizzeria. Abby and I shared an apartment above the pizzeria, but she's married so it's just me up there now. I miss her. We are as close as sisters and complete opposites. She's tall, blonde, and skinny. Where as I'm short, and curvy with dark hair and brown eyes. I look one hundred percent Italian with my olive complexion and Abby favors her father's fair skin. I'm fashion forward while Abby's all jeans and t-shirts. I like a clean house, but Abby is neurotic about it. She's an amazing cook and I burn water. Our living arrangement was great for me, but now I have to clean the apartment and cook for myself.

It sucks.

I get out of the car and get the feeling someone's watching me again. I quickly scan the parking lot. Like before, nothing seems out of the ordinary. A cold shiver runs down my spine. I walk across the parking lot and into the restaurant's kitchen. Being alone in the apartment freaks me out a little, too. Maybe I need a dog.

I mutter as I walked into the kitchen, "Yeah, a really big one would be good."

"That's what we all wish for, honey."

I jump. "Damn it, Marco. Don't sneak up on me!"

"Sorry, honey. Weren't you talking to me?"

"No."

He shrugs. Today, Marco has on black skinny jeans and a bright green *Uncle Dino's* t-shirt. The color looks great against his milk chocolate skin. None of us are sure of Marco's ethnicity other than he declares his mother was a Puerto Rican princess. He stands a few inches taller than my five-foot-two inch frame and probably weighs about a hundred and ten pounds soaking wet. Like me, Marco is very much into fashion—which is why I am appalled when I look at his shoes. On his feet are a pair of bright green Crocs.

"What the hell are those things on your feet?"

Marco winces and holds up his hands. "I know, I know. They are a serious fashion *don't* and are completely hideous, but damn it if they aren't comfortable as hell to wear and my feet don't kill me by the end of the night. Abby got me a pair as a joke a few months ago when the restaurant opened and after one night, I was hooked. Once she found out I liked them, she got them for me in every freaking color they make."

I shake my head. "That's so sad, Marco. Please tell me you don't wear them in public."

He gasps. "Girl, have you lost your mind?" He points to a pair of alligator skin loafers by the door. "At the end of the night, I trade in one croc for another."

Laughing, I grab a plate. "Be right back." I walk through the kitchen and into the pizzeria. I smile as I watch my Uncle Ray and his new wife Carina bicker back and forth. We almost lost Uncle Ray a few months ago when he had a massive heart attack. Luckily Max's father is a heart surgeon and saved him. He was reunited with Carina; the love of his life after her husband died. They eloped once Ray was out of the hospital.

"Se si mangia salsicce che farò tagliare le palle." *If you eat that sausage, I will cut your balls off.* Carina glares at Uncle Ray.

He smirks and kisses her palm. "Allora la mia dolce moglie si vivrà una vita molto insoddisfatto." *Then, my sweet wife, you will live a very unsatisfied life.*

Carina blushes. "One piece and no more."

He grinned and popped the sausage into his mouth. His smile widened when he spotted me. "Bella! What brings you here?"

I lean in and kiss his cheek. Uncle Ray very rarely calls Abby and I by our given names. He calls her *Mio Angelo*; my angel, and me *Bella*; beauty. It's sweet. I have a close relationship with my uncle. He became Abby's guardian when her parents died. She was ten and I was nine. My mother, Abby's mother, and Uncle Ray are siblings. Abby and I were raised by my parents and Uncle Ray, it was really nice. Every childhood memory I have is wrapped up in my family. A Sunday dinner around my mother's dining room table; my dad and Uncle Ray bickering about their favorite sports players. Summer vacations at the Jersey shore. Uncle Ray always let Abby and I bury him up to his waist in the sand. He never complained about the sand in his swimsuit. Instead he would laugh and splash with us in the waves to wash off.

I kiss Carina and casually move the tub with the sausage slices away from Ray. Carina winks at me and turns back to the dough she was working on.

"I came for lunch. Nick is acting like an asino today. I took the afternoon off. What's good today?"

He grabs for the sausage while Carina's back is turned and frowns when his hand met nothing but air. "The sausage was good."

I giggle. "So I've heard. How about a slice with sausage and I'll grab a salad with Marco in the kitchen."

"For you, Bella, anything." Uncle Ray pops a slice into the oven to warm and motions to a seat at the counter. "So what did the asino do? Do I need to talk to him?"

I sat. "No. I took care of him. Work is stressing him out. I understand, but it's not okay to bark orders and treat me like crap."

Uncle Ray tenses. "Did he hurt you?"

"No. Just bruised my ego a little, I guess."

He nods. “I see. I understand what he did was wrong, but you will forgive him, yes? He is working for that obnoxious Glickman woman, no? I met her once and understand why her husband has long office hours.”

I chuckle. “Yeah, Nick calls her *The Dragon Lady*.”

Uncle Ray laughs. “Good one. He is angry with her but takes it out on you? That is not okay but we forgive those we love because we love them.”

“I guess.”

Uncle Ray opens the oven. The smells from the different pizza’s made me grin. Being surrounded by food my whole life, I easily recognize the smell of crusty bread, garlic, tomatoes and basil. Mixed in were the various toppings; onion, pepperoni, sausage, and even peppers. Uncle Ray plates my slice and kisses my cheek. “Go have lunch with Marco. He’ll cheer you up better than I can.”

“Okay. Thanks, Uncle Ray. Bye, Carina.”

She turns and waves. “Ciao, Bella.”

I walk through the kitchen doors and put my plate on the prep table. Marco already made me a salad and set a bottle of water next to my plate.

"What's up, baby cakes?"

I pick at the salad. "Nothing. Nick was an ass to me so I'm taking the afternoon off."

He sits next to me and lays his head on my shoulder. "And?"

I lean into him. "And I'm sad."

"Why, sweetie?"

I sigh. "Marco, is there something wrong with me?"

"What do you mean?"

"Why won't he marry me?"

Marco takes my fork and puts it on the prep table. A tear rolls down my cheek. "Oh, honey, don't cry. He will marry you."

I sniffle. "I'm not so sure."

Marco gathers me in his arms as more tears flow down my face. “Why do you say that?”

“We have been together for three years and nada. I think he’s comfortable with our relationship and doesn’t want to commit. I mean, Abby got married. Uncle Ray got married. Hell, you and James are practically married! Nick and I are stuck and he’s seems fine with it.”

“Have you told him how you feel?”

I nod.

“What does he say?” Marco releases me and hands me a napkin.

I shrug and I wipe my eyes. “He says he likes things as they are and there’s no need to rush.”

Marco snorts. “I think it’s his mother.”

“Maybe. She is bat-shit crazy, but then wouldn’t he want to leave home?”

Marco takes a bite of my pizza and stands. “Maybe he doesn’t want her to feel like both of her boys have run away from her.”

“Maybe.”

NICK

I'm so happy this day is finally over. I didn't hear from Gina for the rest of the day and it kinda pissed me off. I am too tired to go over to her place and fight with her so I head home instead.

After Gina left, I had to get the drunkards out of Mrs. Glickman's house; they were a lawsuit waiting to happen. I wrestled the drunken twins into the truck and brought them to Jesse's place where his girlfriend assured me that he and Alex would be back on the job sober and ready to work tomorrow. Then I had to go back to the site and clean the roses that Alex puked all over. That was fun. Luckily my father showed up and started the tile job in the powder room so Mrs. Glickman wouldn't be all over my ass tomorrow.

I unlock the door to my apartment and sigh. A few years ago my father and I converted the space above my parents' two-car garage into a studio apartment. There is a couch and a fifty-two inch big screen TV as well as a queen sized bed in the space. A small table and two chairs sit against one wall. My 'kitchen' consists of a small countertop with a coffeemaker and microwave on it. There is a small sink and fridge and three cabinets to hold all my culinary needs. We installed a small bathroom with a sink, toilet, and shower. It isn't much, but it is mine.

My mother had visited my place again. My bed is made, the coffeemaker clean, and fresh laundry neatly folded on the corner of my bed.

I'll admit, I have it pretty good. I have my own space, but it's like I still live at home. My mother's a housewife. She's never had a job outside the home. My father, brother, and I are her life. Now that my brother Frank moved to Florida with his wife, my mother shifted twice as much attention to me.

I peel off my grimy clothes, leaving them on the floor, and turn on the shower as hot as it would go. The spray slides over my sore muscles and washes away the day's filth. When the water cools, I turn off the shower and step out. Grabbing a fresh towel, I dry off and wrap the towel around my waist. I head to the fridge to grab a beer.

"I just cleaned this floor and now it's a mess again."

I jump. "Shit, Ma! What the hell?"

She points a finger at me. "Don't you swear at me, young man."

"Sorry, Ma. What are you doing up here?"

She nods to the small table. On it is a covered tray. "Your father said you had a rough day and would probably want to go to bed early. I figured I'd feed you, first."

I wince. What the hell is wrong with me? She is being nice and I yell at her. I kiss her cheek. "Thanks, Ma. You're the best."

She blushes and swats at my arm. "Just leave the dishes in the sink. I'll do them in the morning. You eat, then go to bed."

I sit down to my mother's lasagna as she makes her way to the door. "I put your clothes in the hamper and your wallet on the dresser."

"Thanks, Ma."

Yeah, my life doesn't suck.

***

The next day, true to her word, Mrs. Glickman came to check the progress of the powder room. Luckily Alex and Jesse finished the tile work my dad started the day before and were installing the pedestal sink as she came in.

"Now we're getting somewhere." She looks over the tiled floor and smiles. "I just knew that tile would be fabulous here! Now I think I want to change the wall color."

I groan. Last week we painted the room the color Mrs. Glickman assured us was her 'final choice' and then tiled. It’s always easier to tile after the paint has been put up than the other way around.

“Mrs. Glickman, the room’s already painted. We did it last week, remember?”

She waves at me as if I were a fly. “Oh, but I saw a color yesterday that would be absolutely perfect in here.” She turns and stares at me. “Will it be a problem?”

I open my mouth to tell her exactly what I think when Alex steps in. “Excuse me, Mrs. Glickman, but what color did you have in mind?”

Last week we painted the walls a light dove gray to accent the gray veins that ran within the white marble tiles. The sink and toilet are a pearly white and all the hardware in the room is brushed chrome.

“I saw this wonderful dark plum that would look just lovely in here.”

Alex looks around the room. “Honestly, Mrs. Glickman, I think that would be a mistake.”

She gasps. I scrub a hand down my face.

“Excuse me?”

Alex shrugs. “A color that dark on the walls will make the room seem very small. The light gray makes it feel more spacious. Your guests won’t feel like they are peeing in a coffin. I like the idea of the plum, but wouldn’t it be nicer as an accent color? Maybe use that color for the rug in front of the sink and the hand towels? Just a splash of color goes a long way.”

I hold my breath as Mrs. Glickman looks around the room. “Hmm. I think you’re right. We want light and elegant, not dark and depressing.” She glares at me. “You couldn’t have seen that? I’m glad that this young man is on the job; at least I know *one* of you has some vision and taste.” With that last remark, she turns on her heel and stalks toward the kitchen. “Now what’s going on in here?”

I nod to Alex. “Thanks, man.”

He shrugs. “After yesterday, it’s the least I could do. Go before she fucks up the kitchen.”

GINA

I can't believe Nick didn't call or come over last night to apologize. I fume over the payroll report as I think about Nick. I was so mad this morning, I forgot my lunch on the kitchen counter and my stomach is growling so loud I can't concentrate. I call Uncle Ray about getting something delivered.

"Yeah. Uncle Dino's."

I chuckle. Uncle Ray is never good with the phone. "Hi, Uncle Ray."

"Bella! Two days in a row. What do you need?"

"I forgot my lunch at home and am swamped with paperwork. Is there any way I can get an antipasto salad delivered to the office?"

"For you? Of course! We have a new delivery boy who started today; he'll be there soon."

“Thanks, Uncle Ray.”

“Don’t worry about it and don’t work too hard.”

I hang up the phone and go back to my paperwork. Time must have gotten away from me; I jump when someone knocks on the office door.

“Uncle Dino’s delivery,” the voice calls from the other side of the door.

I rose to unlock the door. I always keep it locked when I was alone. I swing open the door. My jaw hit the floor. “Tommy? Is that you?”

Standing before me is the object of every high school fantasy I ever had. Tommy Reynolds. Damn it if he doesn't look fan-fucking-tastic, too. Tommy was the all-American kid in high school. He stands at least a foot taller than I and his dark hair is cut military short, but what makes me swoon are his crystal blue eyes. I swore they could look into a person’s soul. Tommy was the captain of the football team and every girl wanted him.

“Hey, Gina. How are ya?”

"Good. When did you get back?"

I heard that Tommy was recently discharged from the military, but for the life of me can't remember why. Looking at his beautiful smile, I don't care.

"A few days ago. I went to get lunch yesterday and your uncle mentioned that the regular delivery guy quit. I thought I'd help out till I figure what I want to do."

"That's really sweet, Tommy. It's really great to see you." He smiles as he hands me my salad. "Yeah, you too. So you work for the Zacco's, huh? Do you like it?"

Do I like it? It was something I did after getting my business degree; it was expected, especially since Nick and I were together. I shrug. "It pays the bills."

He nods. "Right, well I've got more food to deliver so I'll see you around." He turns to leave, but quickly turns back. "Gina? I meant what I said. It was really good to see you."

I smile and close the door. I could have sworn I saw heat in his eyes. I shake my head. I need to get laid, but first my idiot boyfriend needs to apologize. I send him a quick text.

Hey. Dinner at my place tonight?

A few minutes later I get an answer.

Sure. Chinese at 8?

Sounds good. I'll get the food, you get the beer?

K

K? That's it? I usually get an ILU—I love you. He better apologize his freaking head off later.

NICK

I lock the door to my red F-150 and grab the beer out of the bed of the truck. I am dirty, tired, and couldn't wait to sink balls deep into Gina.

I plan to do just that after she apologizes for her little stunt yesterday. I use my key to let myself into the private residence door in the back of the pizzeria and head upstairs. Gina left the apartment door unlocked for me. I smell the food as soon as I open the door and my stomach growls.

Gina came out of the kitchen carrying plates and silverware to the table. "Hey." She sets them down and comes over to give me a kiss on the cheek. "Eat or shower?"

"Shower."

Gina nods and goes back into the kitchen. She puts the containers into the microwave to keep warm until I'm done with my shower. I pull out a beer, pop the cap, and take a long pull from the bottle. The cold liquid hits the back of my throat as some of the day's tension rolls off my shoulders. When Gina came back, I'd let her apologize so we can enjoy the rest of our evening. When she came back into the living room, I gesture to the sofa and sit.

"About yesterday."

Gina sits. "Yeah?"

"I'm ready when you are."

She cocks her head to the side and draws her brows together. "Ready for what?"

"Your apology for bringing the boys to the jobsite drunk, acting like a brat, then taking the afternoon off when there was work at the office that needed to be done."

Her eyes narrow. "Are you serious?"

I stand and pace the room. "You're damn right I'm serious. What you did yesterday was completely unprofessional and it made me look bad in front of my crew. I can't have that Gina. I'm your *boss* and that means you will treat me with some damn respect." I stand before her, my hands on my hips. "Are we clear?"

She glared and stood. "Crystal. Get out."

I blink. "What?"

"I said. Get. Out."

I shook my head. "Why?"

She stomps to the door, her back ramrod straight. "Why? *Why?* Oh my God, Nick. Are you that fucking stupid? I was going to let you apologize to *me* for how you acted yesterday. You barked at me like I was a god damn dog. I know you're my *boss,* but that doesn't give you the right to act like a total fucking douchebag!"

"Gina, I'm sorry if you got your feathers ruffled—"

"My feather's ruffled? Are you insane?"

I move around the couch until I am in front of her. "Look, Gina, you have it pretty good at work. I mean, you basically run the office any way you want and my dad and I cater to temper tantrums like the one you pulled yesterday afternoon, but let's be real for a second, shall we? You pull that kind of crap anywhere else and you would be out on your ass like that." I snap my fingers in her face.

Her body shakes with rage. "Tantrum? You want to see a tantrum?" She flings open the door and pushes me into the hallway. "Since you don't know jack shit about what I do at the office and I'm such an unprofessional brat, then I quit!"

My eyes narrow. "Gina, don't say something you don't mean."

She smirks. "Oh I mean it, Nick. I. Quit."

The door slams in my face and the deadbolt clicks into place.

Fuck my life.

GINA

Holy shit, what did I just do? I had a tantrum and quit the best freaking job I've ever had!

I sink onto the couch and sob. I hate crying. I think those women who sit on their couches and eat ice cream because they are depressed are spineless and weak.

Damn it, now I want ice cream.

I go to the freezer and take out the container of my favorite Ben & Jerry's ice cream*; What a Cluster.* I snort at the irony and let the peanut butter ice cream with caramel clusters, marshmallow, and peanut butter swirls ease my pain. After eating the entire pint while watching crappy sitcoms, I still don't feel any better. I need to talk to Abby, but don't want to disturb her on her honeymoon. Sighing I, reach for my phone.

"Hello?"

"Mom?" Just the sound of her voice makes me feel better.

"Tell me what happened."

How does she do that?

"I screwed up big time."

She snickers. "You must have if you're calling me. I'll be over in ten minutes."

I throw out my ice cream container and pull out a bottle of wine and two glasses. I was gulping down my first glass as my mom walks into the living room.

"Starting without me, huh? That's not nice." She pulled me to her chest and I sobbed.

"Okay, let it out and then we'll talk." She leads me to the couch and let me cry on her shoulder for a few minutes. When my tears subsided, I wipe my eyes and face her. "I quit my job today."

She nodded. "Okay."

That is all she says. My mother is the most even-tempered person I know. I guess after living with my dad and having Uncle Ray as a brother, she kinda had to be; *they* are terrible hotheads.

“Don’t you want to know why?”

“Of course I do, honey. Why did you quit your job?”

“Nick was being an asshole to me and I blew up at him and quit.”

She smiles. “So much like your father. What are you going to do next?”

I sigh. “I don’t know. I love my job, but Nick pushed all my buttons in one shot and it really pissed me off, ya know?”

She squeezes my hand, encouraging me to go on.

“I guess he’s right about being the boss and needing the respect of the crew. I understand I’m an employee, but I’m also his girlfriend and didn’t separate the two very well. Damn it, Mom! Nick was right. I had a temper tantrum and quit my job over nothing. *Shit.*”

"Well not exactly nothing, but I think you learned something today. What are you going to do now?"

"I don't know. Definitely a new job. I don't think it's good for our relationship if I keep working for Nick. I'll go in tomorrow and speak to Mr. Zacco."

She pats my leg. "Good girl. Sometimes when you're close to someone it's difficult to take orders from them. Why do you think Angela and I sold our shares of the pizzeria to Ray? We would have killed each other within the first day." She laughs. "Don't worry about a job right now. Give Mr. Zacco your two weeks, then maybe you can help out downstairs until you find something else."

"Thanks, Mom. Having you here and talking it out really made me feel better." She smiles and hugs me. "What are mothers for? I'm just happy to be out of the house. Your crazy father is yelling at the TV again like the characters can hear him."

I laugh for the first time all day.

***

The next morning I went to the office. In one hand I carry a muffin basket and in the other my letter of resignation. I unlock the office door and set the coffee to brew. I am pouring myself some coffee when Mr. Zacco strolls into the office.

“Good morning, Gina. Wow, muffins. What’s the occasion?” He pulls out a banana-nut and takes a healthy bite.

“I’m giving my two weeks' notice.”

He chokes back a laugh, spitting pieces of muffin across the room and rolls his eyes. I hand him the envelope.

“What’s this?” He opens it and reads. His eyes get wider as he reads. “Holy shit, you’re serious?”

I nod, not trusting my voice.

“Why? If it’s money, I might be able to swing a raise your way when the Glickman job is done.”

I shake my head. "It's not about money. It's me and Nick. We snipe at each other too much and he being my boss isn't good for our personal relationship. I'll find someone else and train them before I go; I wouldn't leave without doing that."

He sighs and sits at the table. "I know you wouldn't, you're a good girl. Can I just say that this sucks and I hate the idea of you not being here?"

Tears prick at the corner of my eyes. "Thanks. I love you, too."

He stands and gives me a hug. He holds me tightly, but I'm pretty sure I hear him mutter, "Idiot boy."

When he releases me, his eyes mist over. Clearing his throat, he grabs another muffin and points at me. "Make sure the next person knows I like banana nut muffins and not the bran shit." He turns and walks out, leaving me smiling, but sad.

Sitting at my desk, I quickly type out my job description and post it to a local job website. After working on some contracts for new clients, I decide to check on my post. It is amazing how many responses are in my inbox. Printing off the best two, I send thank you letters to the rest and shut down my computer. The sound of my stomach was gurgling lets me know it is time for lunch.

Popping my head in Mr. Zacco's office, I knock on the door jamb. "Hey. I'm going to *Uncle Dino's,* can I get you anything?"

He gives a mischievous smile. I know exactly what it means. "Uh-uh. The last time you smiled at me like that, your wife called and reamed me out because you didn't eat your dinner that night."

His smile gets wider. "C'mon, Gina, it's the least you can do for me. I'm still heartbroken you're leaving me."

I narrow my eyes and point. "You only get to use that excuse once until I'm gone. This is the way you want to use it?"

He nods, his smile widening.

I huff. “Fine. One personal meat lover’s pizza coming up.”

He rubs his hands together and licks his lips. “Hot damn!”

I am still laughing as I climb into my car.

I pull into *Uncle Dino’s* back parking lot and get out of my car. Taking a deep breath, I shrug off my jacket and throw it on the passenger seat. Spring is in the air and the days are getting warmer.

“Hey, Gina.”

Tommy is heading out the door with several pizza boxes and white food bags. He smiles as he tries to open the hatchback of the delivery car.

“Hang on, let me get that.” I snag the keys hanging off his fingers and hit the key fob. When the locks disengage, I open the hatch. Tommy slides the food into the car with ease and closes the door. “Thanks.”

“No problem. Having fun?”

He shrugs. “Is it weird if I say yes? I mean, I’m basically doing the job meant for a high school kid, but I like it. Ray and Carina are easy to work for and Marco is funny as hell.”

I giggle. “Yeah. They’re a pretty good group. When Abby gets back it’ll even be better; she and Marco are like a well-oiled machine in the kitchen.”

“I can’t wait to see her again. When is she due back?”

I sigh. “Not for another week.”

Tommy gives me a sad smile and looks away. “It sucks to miss someone, doesn’t it?”

“Yeah, but she’ll be back soon.”

Tommy doesn't move, but whispers, “You’re lucky; not everyone comes back.”

I want to ask Tommy if he is alright, but he shakes his head as if coming out of a trance. “Well, I gotta go. Enjoy your lunch. Maybe I’ll see you around.” He holds out his hands for the car keys. “Thanks, Gina.”

"Oh, um. Sure."

He gives me wink, gets into the car, and pulls out of the lot.

What the hell was that and why did I like it?

Marco walks out with a black bag in his hand and a scowl. "Hey, Gina." He detests taking out the trash but always does it when Carina asks him. He lifts the lid of the dumpster, tosses in the bag, and lets go of the lid. He visibly shudders when he turns around. "Bleck."

I laugh. "It's not that bad, you big baby."

"It's horrible and you know it. What are you doing out here all alone?"

I hook my arm through Marco's and smile. "I was talking to Tommy."

An appreciative hum rumbles in Marco's chest. "That boy is F-I-N-E. Not as fine as *my* James, mind you, but he runs a close second."

I giggle. Marco and his boyfriend James Shea just moved in together. Marco's boyfriend is a Philadelphia firefighter—a tall, broad shouldered, well-built African American with a huge heart and a deep melodic voice. He looks a little scary with his clean-shaven head and dark goatee; especially when he wore his sunglasses, which is all the time. Abby and I fell instantly in love when we met him. All he needs is a long leather trench coat and a turtleneck and he can pass as *Shaft's* hotter, younger brother. Despite the menacing looks, he is a giant teddy bear when it comes to Marco and loves him so much.

We sigh, thinking about James.

"I need to talk to Uncle Ray; what's the mood like?"

Marco smiles. "Carina's getting her hair done so he's happy."

I giggle. "Sausage slices?"

Marco's eyes gleam. "Yup, but not too many. I think Carina scares him a little."

I open the door to the pizzeria. "I wouldn't want to mess with her."

Marco bumps my shoulder as he walks past me. "Me either. Is everything alright with you?"

I sigh and sit at the prep table. "Nope. I quit my job this morning."

Marco ties his apron back on and washes his hands. "Why?"

"Nick and I had a fight at work and I—"

"Had a hissy fit and did something rash?"

I pluck a cherry tomato from a bowl on the prep table and pop it in my mouth. "Something like that."

"Can't you get your job back? I'm sure you can *convince* Nick to rehire you." He waggles his eyebrows.

"Marco! Of course I can; I am very *skilled,* you know." I cock an eyebrow at him. "I don't think it's a good idea, though. Lines get blurred and it's hard to separate boyfriend behavior from boss behavior."

Marco chops some Romaine lettuce. “I get that. So what are you gonna do for work?”

I stand and take a deep breath. “I’m gonna go ask Uncle Ray for a job here until I can figure something out.”

Marco stops chopping and claps. “Oh, honey, that’ll be so much fun! Abby will love it, too.”

I smile. “Let’s hope Uncle Ray’s alright with it.”

Marco goes into the walk in refrigerator and comes back with a small pepperoni stick. He hands it to me with a smile.

My eyebrows draw together as I take the pepperoni. “What’s this for?”

Marco grins. “Insurance. Just give it to Ray and he’ll say yes to anything.”

I laugh and give Marco a quick hug. “Thanks, sweetie.”

He hugs back. “Go get ‘em.”

I walk into the pizzeria and smile. Uncle Ray tosses dough in the air as a couple and their children laugh and clap. He makes quite a show, tossing it several times before settling the stretched dough on a pizza pan, adding sauce and all the requested toppings. Uncle Ray pulls out two lollipops from under the counter and gives one to each child. The little boy immediately unwraps the treat and pops it in his mouth, but the little girl tucks it into her pocket as she smiles up at Uncle Ray. My eyes get misty. Uncle Ray is a great dad; he raised Abby after her parents died when she was ten. Still, it is too bad he never had a child of his own. Abby and Max better give him some grandkids soon.

He turns when the family leaves sit and smiles. "Bella! Come` stai?" He grabs my face and kisses both cheeks.

I smile. "I'm okay, I guess."

His eyes narrow as he looks me over. "What's wrong?"

"I quit my job this morning."

He takes a step back, gaze hardening. "Did Nick hurt you? Do your father and I need to sit down with his father?"

I smile and shake my head. “Calm down, Uncle Ray. I quit myself. Nick and I can’t work together anymore. It’s putting a strain on our relationship, so I gave Mr. Zacco my two weeks' notice. I’ll train someone new and I’ll need a new job.”

He crosses his arms over his chest. “You’ll work here.”

“Uncle Ray I—”

“No discussion. You need a job and I have the means to give you one. Done.”

My shoulders sag, the tension rolling off them. “Thank you, Uncle Ray.”

He smiles. “Bella, you and Mio Angelo need only to smile, that’s all the thanks I need.”

I give him a bone-crushing hug. “Uncle Ray, why can’t Nick be more like you and Dad? Even Max is sweet like you.”

Uncle Ray sighs and gives me a gentle squeeze. “I don’t know, Bella, but that boy better open his eyes or he’s going to lose the best thing in his life.” He pulls back and cups my chin with his finger. “Il tuo amore e` un dono.” *Your love is a gift.*

I whisper, “Thanks, Uncle Ray.”

He caresses my chin and claps his hands. “Okay. Are you hungry?”

I laugh and hand him the pepperoni stick. “I need a personal meat lover’s pizza for Mr. Zacco. I’ll grab a salad from Marco.”

Uncle Ray snorts as he reaches for a ball of dough. “Is he going to eat his dinner tonight? That pazzo wife of his called me the last time complaining that he didn’t eat his dinner.”

My jaw hangs open. “Oh my God. She called the office to yell at me, too.”

He chuckles as he works the dough into shape. “Che la donna è fuori di testa.” *That woman is crazy in the head.*

“I know. I don’t know how Mr. Zacco puts up with it.”

Uncle Ray snorts and gives a lascivious smirk.

"Ew! Uncle Ray, gross!"

He shrugs. "What? The crazy ones are usually crazy in *every* room of the house."

I shudder. "Ugh. I'm going in the kitchen now. Call me when the pizza's ready."

Uncle Ray's laughter follows me into the kitchen.

Marco smiles and points to the end of the prep table. He had made me a grilled chicken Caesar salad and poured a glass of Pellegrino with a slice of lemon.

"Thanks, Marco. It looks delish."

He smiles and continues to chop the veggies lined up in front of him. "*Soo* are we gonna be working together?"

I pierce a piece of warm chicken and nod. "Yup. In about two weeks."

Marco claps and does an adorable little fist pump in the air. "Yeah!"

I smile and continue to eat my yummy salad. Tommy comes through the door as I take my last bite. He sees me and saunters over.

“Hey, Gina.”

I give him a wave since my mouth was full. He sits next to me and picks up my glass. My eyes follow as his lips close around my straw and he takes a sip. His eyes never leaving mine, he sits the glass down and winks. “Thanks, I was parched.”

I nodded. “Uh—sure. No problem.”

He stands and nods at Marco. “See ya.” He heads into the pizzeria.

Marco sits in Tommy’s now open seat, mouth hanging open. “Holy fuck. Did it just get hot in here or is it him?”

I reach for my glass and take the straw in my mouth, picturing Tommy’s mouth. “Him. Definitely him.”

“That man wants you.”

I startle. “What? No he doesn’t. He was being flirty, that’s all. He was always like that with the girls when we were in high school.”

Marco snorts and goes back to his veggies. “Girl, a blind man could see he wants you.”

Tommy walks back in carrying a small pizza box. “Ray said this is for you?”

“Um, yeah. It’s my boss’ lunch.” I look at my watch and curse. “I’m late. Thanks, Marco, for the great salad. See ya, Tommy.”

“Not if I see you first.”

I look at Marco, who is fanning himself. He mouths, '*hot.*' I blush and run out the door.

Mr. Zacco is thrilled with his pizza. The rest of the day goes smoothly. I head home with a few resumes to look over for my replacement. The thought of not seeing Mr. Zacco and the guys is starting to depress me. Mix in Tommy and his flirty ways with Nick being an asshole and my head is a complete mess. All I want is a hot bath and a glass of wine.

NICK

“I can’t believe Gina really quit.” I flop into a chair in my parent’s dining room. I usually eat dinner at my place or at Gina’s, but Dad wants to talk about what happened.

“Well, she did. I’ve got her letter of resignation to prove it. She’s going to set up some interviews by the end of the week. What the hell happened?”

I sigh. “I yelled at her and then got pissed when she did what I asked.”

My mother enters with a platter of chicken parmesan and dishes it out. “Well, good riddance to her. I never liked her working there anyway. She is very full of herself.” She heads back into the kitchen before anyone could reply. When she comes back, she sits down the steaming bowl of linguine and sits in her usual place nearest the kitchen. She grabs my plate and scoops some pasta onto it. “She knew too much about the business.”

“Mom, she’s the office manager. It’s her *job* to know what’s going on in the business.”

My mother waves at me as if chasing away a fly. “Nick, do you know who I saw at the market today? Mrs. Lorenzo. Her daughter Amy is still single.”

I choke on my wine. “There’s a reason for that,” I mutter.

Mom looks up from her plate. “What, dear?”

“How nice is that?” I glance at my father his lips twitch.

“I thought maybe you could take her to dinner this weekend?”

“What? Why?”

She sips her wine. “Since that that girl is out of the picture, I thought you and Amy might hit it off.”

I slam my fork down. She doesn't even flinch. “Ma, Gina and I are still together.”

She looks at my father. “But you said . . .”

“I said she quit the company, dear, not Nick.”

Mom sits back and folds her arms across her chest. “You’re still going to see that girl, then?”

Only my mother knows how to push every button I have. “She has a name, Ma. It’s Gina, and yes, I’m still seeing her.”

She huffs, reaching for her glass. “I don’t know why.”

I stand and glare at the woman who gave me life. “I love her! Don’t you understand that?”

She scoffs and stands, mirroring my stance. “You love her? Then why don’t you just marry her and run away like your brother did?”

“Ma, Frank didn’t run away. He got a job in Florida and moved, that’s all.”

“That’s all? That’s *all*? He lets *her* control his life just like *that girl* controls yours!”

Feeling the start of a migraine, I pinch the bridge of my nose. “Ma, just stop it. Frank’s father in law gave him a job in his law firm. He and Rachel moved for the job. Rachel doesn’t control Frank’s life any more than Gina controls mine. I know you don’t like Rachel or Gina, but that’s on you. Frank and I aren’t going to love who you pick out for us! *You* need to stop trying to control us!”

She gasps and falls back into her chair. “Dominic, did you hear what your son just said to me?”

My father cuts a piece of chicken and smiles. “Yup.”

“What are you going to do about it?”

He shrugs and forks up the chicken. “Nothing.”

“Nothing?” She shrieks, making the pain behind my eyes worse.

Dad salutes me with his fork. “Nope. He’s right. Teresa, I love you, but you have to leave the boys alone to follow their hearts.”

She huffs. “I just want what’s best for them.”

My father grabs a piece of bread and slathers some butter on it. “No. You want what’s best for you. Amy is an awful girl and Gina is a great girl. The problem you have with Gina and Rachel is that they are both very strong women who won’t bow to you. Amy wouldn’t sneeze without your permission, which is why you want to push Nick into her arms. Let’s face it, Teresa, your sons chose to be with women who are strong, opinionated, and speak their minds. They are both just like *you.*”

My mom’s scowl deepens with every word my father says. When he is done, she glares at the two of us for what seemed to be an eternity before standing. “I’m going to bed.” She stomps down the hall and slams her bedroom door like a petulant child.

I watch her go and sit back down. “What the hell just happened?” My dad didn't stop eating.

“I don’t know, but could you pass the salad?”

I pass him the salad.

“Thanks. You better eat before it gets any colder.”

I shake my head and let out a snort, but did what he said. It is one of the nicest dinners I've had in my parent's house in a long time.

GINA

I had just settled into the bath when the phone rang. Letting out a string of curses that will send me to confession, I reach over and snatch my cell phone off the toilet tank.

"What," I snap.

"Damn, girl, what the hell crawled up your ass and died?"

Laughing, I apologize. "Sorry, Marco, I was trying to enjoy a nice hot bubble bath with a glass of wine and you called. What's up?"

"I wanted to see if you wanted to go grab a drink, but I'm guessing the answer is no?"

"I'm sorry, sweetie, but no. I want to relax a little tonight. Where's James?"

Marco sighs. “At the firehouse. He has a double shift and I was feeling lonely.”

I giggle. “Maybe you should sext him.”

He chuckles. “Maybe I will.”

“Go for it. If you’re lucky, he’ll call and finish you off with his smooth Barry White voice.”

“Mmm . . . great idea. Gotta go, doll. Bye.”

I laugh and put the phone back. I close my eyes when there is a knock on my door. I try to ignore it, but it just gets louder.

“Seriously? All I want is one freaking night to relax! Do I get that? *Noooooo.”* I grab my robe and hastily knot it at my waist while heading to the door.

“Yeah, yeah. I’m coming.” I pull open the door. “Nick.”

He looks me up and down. “Hey.”

I open the door and step back so he can come in. “What are you doing here?”

He sits on the couch. “I came to talk about why you quit your job.”

I sigh and sit on the opposite side of the couch. Nick frowns.

“Nick, I quit because you and I need some boundaries. The lines between work and play get blurred when we’re together. I got some promising leads for your father, though, and I’ll train my replacement before I go.”

He sighs and scrubs the back of his neck. “I guess it’s for the best.”

Wow. I don't know why, but I kinda want him to fight my decision.

“Is that all you wanted to talk about?”

He shifts in his seat. “Why? You looking to get rid of me?”

“No, it’s been a long week and I was in the tub when you knocked. I wanted to relax and go to bed early tonight.”

“Oh. Go have your bath and then I’ll tuck you in.”

I sigh. He doesn't get it. “Okay.”

I get up and shuffle to the bathroom. I go in and lock the door behind me. All the pretty candles lit around the room and the abandoned glass of wine on the sink mock me. Dumping the wine down the sink, I sigh and blow out the candles. I let the water out of the tub and take a quick shower instead.

About twenty minutes later, I reenter the living room to see that Nick had made himself at home. He randomly kicks his shoes off on the way to the kitchen, leaving dirt clumps on the rug. A bottle of beer sweat all over my antique coffee table. ESPN blares on the TV and Nick is fast asleep on the couch. I snatch the bottle off the table, mopping up the water with the corner of my robe, hoping it won't leave a ring. I have coasters on the table for a reason, but no matter how many times I tell Nick to use one, he never does. I turn off the television, dump the beer down the kitchen sink, and go to bed.

My alarm startles me out of a sound sleep. I grope the bedside table to shut it off. I look around my room. Nick never came to bed last night. I pad out to the living room. The couch is empty.

I walk into the kitchen and gasp.

It is a mess. There are coffee grinds all over the counter and floor. A bowl of half-eaten cereal and a used coffee cup sit in the bottom of the sink. There is a loaf of bread on the counter next to an open butter container. I go to put the lid on the butter and it is full of toast crumbs. I dig them out with a spoon and shove the butter back in the fridge. I grab the milk for my coffee and give the container a shake. Grabbing my favorite mug, I pour barely a teaspoon of milk into my coffee and curse. Why did he put it back with so little left?

Now I am pissed. Nick knows I need my coffee before heading to the gym. I clean up the kitchen and go to brush my teeth where another surprise waits for me. Globs of toothpaste dot the sink and counter. After cleaning up yet another mess, I grab my toothbrush. It is wet. Upon closer inspection, I see toast crumbs on the bristles.

"Motherfucker!"

He used my toothbrush? Who does that?

I throw it away and reach for a new one under the sink, only to realize that I don't have any more.

"Damn it!"

I wash my face and throw my hair into a ponytail. I brush my teeth as best as I can with my finger and stomp into my bedroom. I put on my gym clothes, grab my work clothes, and head out to my car.

I am late to the gym because I spent my morning cleaning up after my jerk boyfriend and miss my spin class. The only machine open is the dreaded treadmill. With my iPod blasting 80's classics I pay no attention to the presence next to me. I don't go to the gym to make friends or be social. I go to keep myself in shape. My cousin Abby is naturally skinny with big boobs. That bitch can eat anything and not gain an ounce. I punch up the speed on the treadmill. I'm not so lucky. Oh I got the big boobs, but I also have the hips and ass to go with them. I work out five days a week because I like to eat. If I didn't work it off, I'd look like Jabba the Hut.

I hit the cool down button and slow my pace. When the treadmill stops, I grab my water bottle and take a long healthy swig.

"Hey."

I almost jump at the voice next to me. Tommy. "That was a fierce pace you were running. I had a hard time keeping up."

I wipe the sweat off my brow with a towel and look him over. His white t-shirt stretches tight across his chest and arms. Little black lines from a tattoo peak out from under both sleeves. The blue basketball shorts ride low on his hips. There is a scar on his right leg running from under his sock to just above the knee.

He clears his throat and chuckles when I blush. "That looks like it hurt."

His smile disappears. "It did. I'm lucky I got to keep my leg and my life."

My heart twists. "I haven't seen you here before. Did you just join?"

His smile returns. "Yeah. I miss the routine of the daily workouts I had to do in the Marines. Now that I'm stateside again, I wanted to get some of that back."

I nod. "That's great." We walk across the gym to get the cleaner to wipe down our machines. After we are done, we walk back to throw out the paper towels and head to the Sani station to wash our hands. Tommy never leaves my side.

"Do you usually come here in the mornings?"

I wash my hands. "Yeah. I usually take a spin class, but I was running late this morning so I had to use the treadmill instead."

Tommy stops to retie his sneaker. "Why were you late?"

I don't know what comes over me, but I end up telling Tommy everything. "Then he used my tooth brush and since it was my last one, I had to brush my teeth with this." I hold up my index finger. "It was gross." I feel foolish. “I’m sorry, Tommy. I didn’t mean to unload all that crap on you so early in the morning. It’s Abby’s fault, really. If she were home, I would have called her and complained, but she won’t be back for a few more days.”

Tommy and I walk to the locker room doors. “It’s alright, really. I’m a good listener and if you need a shoulder” —he points to his— “I’ve got two you can use.”

I blush. “Thanks, Tommy.”

He smiles and holds up a finger. “Stay here for a sec.”

He dashes into the men’s locker room, returning a few minutes later with a little travel kit. “Here. I always keep a spare in my gym bag for emergencies.”

I look down; there is a toothbrush and small tube of toothpaste in my hands. “Oh, Tommy, you’re a life saver!” I kiss his cheek, stepping back quickly, my face flush. “Sorry. I gotta go, but thanks.” I turn and flee into the ladies locker room.

NICK

My day starts off with a bang. After leaving Gina's, I head home to change and run into my mother. Of course she knows I didn't sleep at home and mutters something about 'that puttana,' but I don't stop to listen. How is it that I'm a grown ass man, but my mother makes me feel like a guilty child in the matter of seconds? I change my clothes, grab the cooler my mom packs my lunch in, and get to the jobsite just in time to meet Mrs. Glickman.

Great.

"I see the kitchen is coming along nicely." She walks over and runs her polished nails over the new black granite countertop. "Are you still scheduled to finish on time?"

I refrain from rolling my eyes. "Yes, ma'am."

She spins on her pencil-thin heels and walks to the completed powder room. "Good. I do love the plum accents in here. I’m so glad I didn’t let you paint the walls this dark color like you wanted to.”

I grasp my hammer and take a deep breath. “Uh-huh.” I don't want the stupid purple color and she knows it, but Mrs. Glickman doesn’t like to look foolish and if I argue she’ll just stay longer. I need her to leave before she ends up with my hammer between her eyes.

“I have a tennis lesson in an hour, but I will be back later to check on all of you.”

As soon as she is gone, I go over the punch list for today. Jesse and Alex come in a few minutes later and we go over the list of what needs to be completed by the end of the day. As soon as everyone is situated, I call Gina.

“Good morning. Zacco Construction, how can I help you?”

“Hey, babe. How’s your morning been?”

She sighs. “It would have been better if I got to the gym on time for my spin class.”

“That sucks. Why were you late? Slept in?”

“No. I had to spend the morning cleaning up your mess. Honestly, Nick, you’re a pig.”

I am confused. “Mess? What mess?” My apartment is always clean. What the hell is she talking about?

“Let’s see. There was the open loaf of bread left on the counter, the toast crumbs in the butter, the half-eaten bowl of cereal in the sink, the coffee grounds all over the place, and the teaspoon of milk left in the container. Not to mention the glob of toothpaste in the bottom of the bathroom sink and you used my toothbrush! Who does that?”

I guess I did leave the apartment a little messy, but no big deal, right?

“Sorry, babe, but you got it all cleaned up, right, so no big deal?”

“No big deal? Nick, it’s not my job to clean up after you. I’m not your mother.”

I know where this is going. We have this argument *a lot*.

“Gina, leave my mother out of this.”

“Are you kidding? The whole reason you’re a slob is because she comes in and cleans up after you on a daily basis. For fuck’s sake, Nick. When the hell are you going to grow up?”

“You’re one to talk,” I mumble.

“Excuse me?”

“Seriously, Gina, you’re gonna point fingers? You live above your uncle’s business and have it pretty good in terms of rent.”

“At least I pay rent. I’m also responsible for utilities and cleaning up after myself. This includes cooking, cleaning, and even laundry! Do you know how to wash your clothes, Nick?”

Silence. What can I say to that? I don't know how to work the damn washer. It’s not my job to know that shit.

“That’s what I thought. Look, I hope you don’t think my sole purpose in life is to marry you and pick up where your mother leaves off. That isn’t happening, buddy.”

“What the hell does that mean?”

"That means, if we get married I'm still going to work. You *will* pitch in around the house, which includes the cooking *and* the cleaning. Also, if you think I'm going to stand by and allow your mother to go all Marie Barrone, you're sadly mistaken."

"Marie Barrone?"

"Yup. She won't be popping over whenever she feels like it. She won't be giving me cooking or cleaning tips. And she sure as shit won't have a key to the house."

Damn. "I didn't realize how much you hated my mother."

She sighs. "I don't hate her, Nick but she's intrusive as hell and hasn't let you grow up. You're days living like Peter Pan are numbered. It's time to grow up, little boy."

I am pissed. "Peter Pan? Are you fucking kidding me? I'm a grown up, Gina. I run a damn business, don't I?"

She laughs. "Nick, your dad and I run the business. You do run the crew, but you don't know shit about the business beyond that. You think you're a grown up? Stay over at my place on Saturday night."

"I can't."

"Tell me why again, Nick?"

"Because," I say through clenched teeth. "My mom makes me a special breakfast on Sunday morning before we go to mass."

"Mm-hmm. And your dad?"

"He goes to Saturday night mass."

"And mommy doesn't go with him, why?"

I sigh. "She likes to have her special Sunday mornings with me."

"Right. So you can't spend Saturday night with me because mommy will be upset, right? Jesus, Nick, you're not a baby. Your mother needs to cut the damn cord already."

She is right. I know she is right, but damn if I am going to admit it. “Listen, Gina, I gotta go. Am I gonna see you later?”

“No. I want to take the bath I never got to take last night. I’ll just talk to you tomorrow.”

“Fine.” I hang up.

I rub at the pain swirling in my chest. Why does it feel like I am losing her?

GINA

Idiot. Nick needs to wake the hell up and realize that if things don't change, we're done.

Wow. I think that is the first time I admitted that to myself. Let's face it; I'm not getting any younger. If I want kids someday, I want to be young enough to enjoy them. I can't raise Teresa Zacco's son while trying to raise my own kids.

A knock on the door broke me from my thoughts. At least he is on time. I like punctuality for an employee.

Opening the door, I am greeted by Edward Wilson. He is fresh out of college and looking for a job that will put his business degree to good use. He looks nervous, but smiles while grasping my hand in a firm shake. He is tall with blonde hair that is a little shaggy but seems to be all the rage this year and green eyes. His rimless glasses make him look older. He wears pressed khakis and a navy blue sports coat over a crisp white dress shirt. No tie. I like the look; it is young but still professional.

"Good afternoon, Miss Toriello. I'm Edward Wilson. We had an appointment?"

He has the most delicious British accent. "Yes. Please come in, Mr. Wilson. Call me Gina."

"Only if you call me Edward."

He follows me into the office and waits until I sit before unbuttoning his sports coat and sitting.

"Why do you want to work for Zacco construction?"

He smiles. He has nice straight teeth. "I'm new to the area and found the thought of a local business more alluring than a big business."

"I see. May I ask where you're from?"

"New York. I've lived there with my mum since I was a teenager."

"What made you move to Chester Springs?"

He gives a sheepish grin. "It's a cliché, but I moved for love. My fiancé is from here. Jessica Duffy? Her parents own the bakery in town."

"Jessica and I went to high school together. She's a great girl and her parents are so sweet."

He blushes. "Thanks. Jessica said she liked you, too."

"Tell me what you know about structuring a business."

For the next fifteen minutes, Edward impresses me with his knowledge of the office system we use. He even shows me an easier way to streamline payroll and our accounts. I am impressed as hell, but he still needs to win over Mr. Zacco.

"So far, Edward, I'm impressed with your skills, but I'm not sure if you can handle our suppliers and customers. They like to play hardball. I can usually manipulate what I want, being a girl and all, but for you . . . ." I shrug.

He laughs. "Gina, I assure you that I can handle anything you throw at me. My mother manages a *very* successful hedge fund in New York. I've learned from the best."

"Okay, let's test your skills, shall we?" I reach into a drawer and hand him a red folder. He opens it and scans the contents.

"This family hasn't paid for their custom-built fireplace that was installed six months ago?"

I nod. "They claim they don't have the money."

He scans the paperwork once more. "Hmm. Do you mind if I use the computer for a moment?"

I stand and we switch seats. A few keystrokes later, he picks up the phone. "Good afternoon, Mr. Parker? Yes my name is Edward Wilson and I work with Miss Toriello and Mr. Zacco. Yes, I'm calling in regard to the money owed for your fieldstone fireplace." He nod as he listens. "Yes, sir, I understand that you claimed bankruptcy and cannot pay the balance for the fireplace. I also see from your daughter's Facebook page that your family recently went to Aruba for a month? I wonder how the IRS would deal with that information . . . . I am not threatening you at all, sir, just speculating out loud . . . . Of course if you can't pay then we have no problem coming over and removing the fireplace stone by stone." He pauses for a few moments; a smile spreads over his face. "Excellent, sir! I'll let them know that we can expect payment by the end of business tomorrow. Oh and, Mr. Parker? Either cash or a cashier's check, please; your personal check will not be acceptable. Thank you so much. Goodbye."

I sit there with my mouth hanging open. "Oh. My. God. That was amazing to watch! You just stuck it to him and with your accent; it sounded so damn polite."

He chuckles as we switch seats. "Like I said, I learned from the best."

"Well, I'm impressed as hell."

The door opens. Mr. Zacco appears in my doorway. "Hey, Gina."

I smile and stand, gesturing to Edward. "Mr. Zacco, I'd like to introduce you to Edward Wilson—my replacement."

Edward stands and shakes Mr. Zacco's hand. "Pleasure to meet you, sir."

"Sir? Son, if you're gonna work here, you're gonna need to cut that shit out right now." He turns to me. "What makes you think he can do your job?"

I shrug. "His fiancée is Jessica Duffy, he has a business degree from Manhattan College, and he's already made improvements to the payroll system."

Mr. Zacco looks over at Edward. "That right?"

Edward simply nods.

"Oh and the best part? Edward just got the Parkers to pay their balance."

Now I have Mr. Zacco's attention. He turns to Edward. "Really? How'd you manage that?"

Edward shrugs. "I simply pointed out a few things the IRS might be interested in that I would keep quiet about if Mr. Parker paid his balance in full by the end of business tomorrow. Cash or bank check only; this way he can't stop payment after he leaves the office."

Mr. Zacco crosses his arms over his chest. "You blackmailed him?"

Edward puts his hands in his pockets. "Blackmail is an ugly word. I just made him aware of his options. Personally, I think he made the right choice."

Mr. Zacco doesn't move for a few minutes. He just stares at Edward. Slowly his face splits into a huge grin. "Well, damn, Eddie. Welcome aboard! Oh and we're casual around here." He points to his outfit. "Jeans are fine." He turns to walk out, but spins around suddenly. "Please tell Jessica I like the banana nut muffins. I expect muffins every Monday morning. Get what you like in addition to the banana nut, unless it's bran. I hate that shit. Gina will show you where the petty cash is." He walks away, muttering about his new British enforcer.

Edward and I wait until Mr. Zacco closes his office door before we bust out laughing. We make plans for Edward to start the following day. If all goes smoothly, I won't need to stay past the end of the week.

NICK

I sigh as I open my lunch. Mom made me a bologna and cheese sandwich. There are also grapes and a pudding cup. She also packed water and a Yoohoo. I eat like a goddamn five year old. I think about the lunches Abby made for my buddy Max and sigh again.

Gina is right; I am fucking Peter Pan.

"What's up, boss?" Jesse and Alex sit with me on the front steps and open their lunches. Jesse has a turkey sub. Alex a BLT. I am jealous of their lunches.

"Nothing. I guess I should tell you that Gina quit."

They stop chewing gape at me with confused frowns. Jesse recovers first. "No shit? Why?"

"It's complicated."

Alex nods. "Yeah, it's hard to date the boss."

"Yeah? What do you know about it?"

Alex sips his iced tea. “Before I started here, I worked for a roofer in Jersey. His daughter was the office manager.” He shrugs. “We'd dated for a few months when her father made her choose—me or the job.”

Jessie snorts. “Prick.”

I agree. “That’s tough. I’m sorry, Alex.”

Alex stares down at his sandwich. “She picked me. She told her dad and he flipped out. They had a huge argument. She ran out of the house. She called me as she was driving to my apartment. It was raining . . . . She never made it.”

Jessie whispers, “Fuck.”

I stare at Alex. “Shit, man. That sucks. I’m so sorry.”

Alex stares out into the yard and nods. “She was amazing. Funny, smart, and caring.” He clears his throat and shrugs. “So yeah I get the stress of dating the boss. Gina did the right thing.” He gets up, tossing his sandwich into the trash, and heads back to work.

Jesse and I watch him go. Jesse lets out a breath. "Damn, it makes sense now."

"What does?"

Jesse's eyes never leave the door Alex walked through. "The sadness he deals with. He only goes out on Saturday nights after he comes back from spending the afternoon in Jersey. I think he goes to the grave every weekend."

"Damn."

Jesse nods. "The shitty part? He's a really great guy. My girlfriend tried to fix him up a few times, but he refuses. Someday I hope he'll be ready to move on, because right now, he's not living."

Jesse closes his lunch bag and follows Alex inside. I sit thinking about what Jesse said. In a way, I am like Alex. I'm not going forward with my life either. I am twenty-five years old and have been with Gina for three years. I know I love her so what the hell am I waiting for? Gina wants a family and to be honest I do too. The thought of kids made me grin like an idiot. I need to make more of an effort with the business, too. My dad wants to retire in a few years and I need to step up my game if I am going to take over the company.

GINA

Mr. Zacco and I are impressed with Edward's quick grasp of the business. I decide to leave my job a few days earlier than expected.

"Just because you don't work here anymore doesn't mean you're allowed to forget about my special pizza, got it?" Mr. Zacco gives me a tight hug. When he finally lets go, I put the last of my personal items from my desk in a box.

I chuckle. "Yeah, yeah. I'll even deliver it myself."

I know this is the only way I'd get to see Dominic. Nick's mom doesn't really like me so I am never invited to Sunday dinner or anything.

He pulls back and places a kiss on my temple. "You really are a good kid."

Blushing, I smile at Edward. "If you need anything, just call."

He nods. "Thanks."

I grab my box and head to my car. About a block away from the office, I pull into an empty parking lot and cry my eyes out. I am happy to have a job with Marco and Abby, but the guys are family too. My chest hurts from the loss.

It takes about twenty minutes for me to get myself composed before I head back out on the road.

When I get home, I head into the pizzeria rather than upstairs to my empty, quiet apartment. Marco is busy at the prep table making salads for the customers in the restaurant. My mother stirs what smells like her famous marinara sauce on the stove.

Marco smiles as I snag a cherry tomato. "Hey, sweetie! Go wash your hands and be useful, would ya?"

I kiss my mother on the cheek and head to the sink. "Busy tonight?"

Marco shrugs as he juliennes a carrot. "The usual, not too bad."

Mom scoffs. "Not too bad? I'm exhausted. I'm so glad Max and Abby are coming home tomorrow. I hate missing my shows."

I chuckle. Mom is a talk show junkie. She has her little routine every day, which includes housework, *The View, Dr. Oz,* and *Dr. Phil*. She has a DVR, but says it isn't the same as watching it "live." I tried to explain that the shows are taped in advance, but she doesn't care.

I help Marco plate the salads before putting them into the walk-in fridge. Grabbing a large metal mixing bowl and a small whisk, I use the extra virgin olive oil, red wine vinegar, minced garlic, salt, pepper, basil, and oregano to make *Mio Angelo's* house dressing. I hate to cook. Even though I will never be a chef like Abby, I hold my own when I have to. Mom and Abby taught me some basic dishes. I don't cook too much for Nick for two reasons. One, I don't want to be compared to Abby. Two, he will expect me to cook the meal, serve him, and do the dishes after working all day. No thank you.

Marco dips his pinky in the bowl to taste my dressing as I whisk and smiles. “Nice job, Hun. Abby’s gonna be so psyched that you’ll be helping us here.” He bumps my hip. “I know I’m psyched. In fact, I got you a present.”

I stop whisking and clap my hands. “A present? Where is it?”

I love presents. Mom chuckles while Marco hands me a box with a giant purple bow on top.

I gasp when I open the box. “Oh no. Are you freaking kidding me? This is a joke, right?”

I hold up the dark blue Crocs, wrinkling my nose in disdain. “I’m not wearing these, Marco.”

He pats my shoulder. “Just give them a chance. I swear, after one night you’ll thank me.”

“He’s right, Gina.” She proudly lifts her leg to show off her offensively bright orange shoes. “I love these damn things. The first night I worked here, I went home and my knees and back were killing me. Marco gave me these the next day and" —she snaps her fingers— "no more pain."

"Seriously, Mom? Orange?"

She shrugs. "If they're good enough for Mario Batali, they're good enough for me."

I look from Marco to my mother; their hopeful smiles breaking my resolve. "Fine, I'll try them tomorrow when I start my first shift."

Marco claps and gives me hug. "Wait 'til Abby sees you in them."

I groan.

***

The next morning I decide to sleep in and skip the gym. I am enjoying a very dirty dream starring Ryan Gosling when something pounces on my bed.

"Get up, you lazy ass. I'm home!"

I crack one eye and bolt up when Abby's face smiles back at me. "Holy shit! When did you get here?" I stop and sniff. "Do I smell coffee and bacon?"

She hops off my bed. "Yup. I made breakfast and if you want any you better get your ass outta that bed." She skips out of my room.

I jump out of bed and head to the kitchen. I stop short when I see Max at the table. "Hey, Max."

Max is truly hot—tall with broad shoulders, short sandy brown hair, and striking green eyes. He is in amazing shape and worships the ground my cousin walks on. As if the looks aren't enough; he is smart, sweet, thoughtful, and funny. The total package.

He gives me an amused grin as he sets down his coffee mug. "Hey, Gina. Nice outfit."

I am still in my PJs, which consists of a pair of hot pink boy shorts and matching camisole, sans bra. Most women would be embarrassed with a man they aren't sleeping with seeing them dressed this way, but I'm not most women.

"Thanks." I snag a mini muffin and join him at the table. "So how was the honeymoon?"

I am treated to a full face smile as he looks to where Abby is in the kitchen. "Amazing." He looks so damn happy.

Abby comes into the room with plates of eggs and bacon. She puts down the plates and kisses her husband. "What are you talking about?"

I help myself to the bacon. "Max was telling me what a sex fiend you've become. I'm so proud." I set my fork down, wiping an imaginary tear from my eye. "*Mio Angelo* is a true pervert now."

She smacks me with a dish towel and laughs. "Jealous?"

I reach for the eggs. "Terribly. I've had quite the dry spell lately. Nick and I haven't had sex since you left."

Max grunts and stands. "On that note, ladies, I'll be going." He bends and kisses my cheek. "Gina, always a pleasure." He then grabs Abby by the waist and dips her. The way he attacks her mouth made me all hot and bothered by the time they are done. Max stands Abby upright. She gives him a coy smile. "Not bad, Mr. Harris."

He gently smacks her ass. "Not bad? Guess I'll have to step up my game later." He winks as she turns the cutest shade of red and heads out the door.

Abby's eyes never leave Max until the door closes behind him. She shakes her head, sitting down. "Why haven't you been having sex?"

"Back it up sister; does he always kiss you like that?"

She blushes deeper as she sips her coffee.

"Damn, Abby. You are one lucky bitch."

She sighs. "I know. Now tell me, why have you been celibate?"

"Mrs. Glickman."

Abby sits up straight in her chair. "What? Nick's sleeping with Mrs. Glickman?" Her eyes are wide.

I shake my head. “No, you dumbass. He’s working on her house and she’s being a royal pain in the ass.”

“Oh. That sucks.”

“I know. We’ve had a few fights lately. One of them got pretty bad and I quit my job.”

Abby stands and paces the room. “You quit? Quit your job? Gina, that’s crazy! Are you still dating Nick? What did Mr. Zacco say? Do I need to kick Nick’s ass? What are you going to do for money? Never mind that, you can work downstairs. What was I thinking? I’ll talk to Uncle Ray for you—”

She paces faster and faster with each question. I grab her wrist. “Abby, stop. You’re making me nauseous with the pacing and diarrhea of the mouth.” She blinks and opens her mouth. I hold up my hand to silence the next barrage of questions. “Sit down and I’ll fill you in.”

Over breakfast I tell Abby about everything. She doesn't say a single word until I am done.

“Holy shit, Gina.”

I sigh. "Yeah, but it'll be okay. Tomorrow is Nick's last day on the Glickman job and then hopefully everything will go back to normal."

After breakfast, Abby goes to run errands before we met at the restaurant for work. I do laundry and catch up on bills. It is nice to have a day to breathe.

Around one o'clock, I take a shower and put on a pair of jeans and a dark blue t-shirt. I grab my new footwear from the closet and slip my manicured toes in. The sensation is weird at first, but as I walk across my apartment, I find I don't hate the way my feet feel.

Damn it. I will never live this down.

I throw my hair into a ponytail and put on some mascara and lip gloss. I smile at myself in the bathroom mirror and head downstairs.

As soon as I enter the kitchen, Abby pounces on me; she grabs my arm, throws me into the walk-in fridge and slams the door behind us. I would have panicked, but I know there is a safety handle on our side of the door so we can't get locked in.

Abby turns and points her finger in my face as she hisses. "Tommy Reynolds works here now? You didn't tell me that this morning!"

"Shit, sweetie. I forgot! I'm so sorry."

Abby had a terrible crush on Tommy in high school. He made the mistake of coming up behind her one day in the hallway and grabbed her arm; she had dropped her Biology notebook and he was trying to give it back to her. Abby was training to be a black belt in karate at the time and her instincts kicked in. She grabbed Tommy's arm and almost broke his wrist. Needless to say, he didn't go anywhere near Abby for the next two years. She was crushed. Her actions had every guy in school too scared to ask her out.

"Damn it, Gina. What the hell am I going to do?"

I rub my arms to ward off the chill. "Abby, it was high school. Let it go."

She shakes her head and looks down. I see a smile form on her face. "Gina?"

I rub my arms a little harder. It is freakin' cold in here. “Yeah?”

She giggles and points. “What have you got on your feet?”

I groan. “Shut up. Marco gave them to me as a *welcome to the kitchen* gift yesterday. At least they aren’t bright orange like the ones he got my mom.”

Abby holds her stomach as she laughs. “Oh my God. Where’s my phone?”

I glare at her, pointing my finger. “No pictures, Abby. I mean it.”

She tries to give me a serious look, but fails miserably. “Okay, no pictures, but everyone’s going to know when you deliver salads in the restaurant tonight.”

I feel my stomach drop. “You wouldn’t.”

She giggles and opens the door. The warm air from the kitchen warms me up instantly. “Welcome to the kitchen, Gina.”

She walks out and grabs her apron.

I sigh, grab a few salad plates on my way out.

Bitch.

NICK

Halle-fucking-lujah! I sign off on the finishing touches for the Glickman house. My smile fades as the clicking of heels that I swear have haunted my dreams for the last five weeks grow louder. Mrs. Glickman came into the kitchen with Dr. Glickman trailing behind her. She and Pookie wear matching blue sweaters today.

I hate that stupid dog.

"Well, dear, what do you think? I think the boys did a great job." Dr. Glickman pushes his Buddy Holly styled glasses up his nose. He is a skittish man around his wife.

Mrs. Glickman has yet to speak a word. Her shoes *click-clack* over the tiled floor as she surveys the room. She runs a fingertip across the dark granite countertop and rubs imaginary dust from her fingers.

"It's very nice. I hoped it would be done sooner, but that point is moot now, I suppose."

Don't kill her.

Dr. Glickman clears his throat. "Dearest, they did finish a week ahead of schedule." He gives me a shaky smile.

Mrs. Glickman opens and closes the light cherry cabinets to the right of the new white porcelain farmer's sink—complete with adjustable stainless pot faucet. "Yes, I suppose they did. Hopefully there's no lack of quality work as a result."

Don't kill her.

I clear my throat. "Well, if you're satisfied, then I'll need a signature on this invoice and we'll be done here." I hand the pen to Dr. Glickman. His hand shakes as he looks at his wife. "Dearest?"

She waves her hand. "Sign it."

Dr. Glickman lets out an audible sigh as he signs the invoice. I take the paperwork and pen and hand them to Mrs. Glickman.

She looks at me as if I scratched my ass in public. "What?"

“The paperwork requires your signature, as well.”

She narrows her eyes. “Why? You have his already.” She waves her hand in her husband’s direction. “You don’t need mine.”

I give a tight smile. “Company policy. Both residents need to sign so no one can come back at the company later saying we didn’t complete the job.”

It isn't really company policy, but I don't want any more shit from this woman. I don't trust her as far as I want to throw her.

She huffs and snatches the pen and paper from my hand. “Fine.” She scrawls her signature under her husband's and thrusts everything back at me. “There. Happy?”

I give her a genuine smile. “Absolutely.” Sticking the paperwork in my back pocket, I give Dr. Glickman a sympathetic nod as he hands me a check, and head out the door.

***

"I swear to God, babe, all I wanted to do was smack the shit out of her."

Gina reaches around me and grabs a plate from Marco. "Uh-huh."

She walks out of the kitchen as I snag a salad from the fridge. I am pouring dressing on it when Gina comes back in. "Hey, do you want to go get a beer with me and Max tonight?" I grab a roll from a nearby bread basket, which earns me a glare from Gina. "What?"

She sighs as she replaces the roll. "Nick, I'm working. I can't go get a beer with you."

I roll my eyes. "Sure you can. Abby won't mind."

Gina glares at me. "Nick. I'm. Working."

I stand, wiping my mouth. "Whatever, Gina. If you don't want to spend time with me, just say so."

She throws her hands in the air. "Are you serious? I can't win here, can I? I quit my job at your company because we were fighting. I get this job and we're still fighting. I'm screwed no matter what I do!"

I grin and whisper, “If you come with me, I can guarantee you’ll get screwed.”

Marco snorts, but keeps his eyes trained on the dishes he is plating. Gina's face grows red, but she isn't blushing.

She is pissed.

“Nick, you need to go. Go out with Max. I’ll call you tomorrow.”

Now I am pissed. “Seriously? I just finished five weeks in hell. All I want to do is celebrate with my girl and you’re blowing me off?”

Gina sighs and throws her hands in the air. “For the last time, Nick, I’m *working,* not blowing you off.”

I throw the napkin on the salad plate. “Whatever, Gina. I’ll call you tomorrow."

GINA

As soon as Nick walks out, I throw my dishtowel across the room. "*Agh*! What is wrong with him?"

Abby squeezes my shoulder. "Don't worry, sweetie, Max'll straighten him out."

I sigh and wipe away a stray tear. "Thanks, but Max doesn't need to fight my battles. Besides, Nick shouldn't need to be straightened out about this. He acted like a spoiled brat. I'm really getting tired of it."

Someone behind me clears their throat. I turn. Tommy held out the towel I threw. "I think you dropped this." He smiles.

I snatch the towel from him.

Tommy's smile drops. "Tommy, I'm not mad at you. Nick and I just had an argument and I'm still upset with him. I shouldn't have taken it out on you. I'm sorry."

His smile returns. I can't help but smile. “If you were mine, I’d devote all my time to keeping that smile on your face.” He nods at Abby and Marco and heads into the pizzeria.

I turn around. Abby holds the big knife, her arms crossed and a scowl on her face. “What the hell was that?”

Marco adds his two cents. “That’s what he does, flirts with her.”

Abby points the scary knife at me. “Watch your ass, Gina Lucia Toriello. I mean it.”

I give her a mock salute. “Yes, ma’am.” I pick up the plate and fork Nick abandoned on the prep table and get back to work.

NICK

“Can you believe that shit?” I take a long pull from my beer.

“Dude, did you think she’d drop everything and go because you wanted her to? She was working, Nick.”

Scowling at Max I look around at my friends to back me up. Jesse and Alex shake their heads.

“Seriously, dude, that’s kinda messed up.”

Alex nods in agreement.

“Shut up, Jesse.” I take another pull and signal the waitress for another round.

Jesse glances at Max. “How was Italy?”

“It was good. We didn’t get out much.” He winks. Jesse and Alex crack up.

I shake my head. “Why spend all that money just for a bed? Hell, you could have done that here.”

Alex shakes his head. “Nick, do you understand romance at all, you cheap motherfucker?”

I snort. “Romance? What Max was doing wasn’t romantic. It was instinct.”

Max points his beer bottle at me. “You’re an idiot my friend. Our trip was nothing but romance. The sex was a bonus.”

“Whatever. What am I going to do about Gina?” I look around the table.

“Apologize.”

“Beg.”

“Grovel.”

The waitress drops off our drinks. I take my fresh beer and drink half of it in one swallow. “Fuck that.”

Max stands and throw money on the table. “I’m going to get my wife and be *instinctual*.” He points at me.

"Consider your next move with Gina very carefully, dude. It could be your last."

Jesse and Alex stand and add to the pile of money. "We're going, too."

I nod. "Take tomorrow off. After the weeks we spent in Glickman hell, we earned it. Well, except for Max, that is." I laugh at my own joke.

"Boss, are you going to be alright?"

Max snatches my keys. He walks over to the bartender and they exchange a few words. The bartender looks over at me then nods at Max.

"Dude, did you take my keys?"

He stares down at me. "You can't drive. I told Mike to call you a cab when you're done. Jesse will drive your truck home and Alex will follow to take him home." He hands my keys to Jesse.

I am pissed. "Since when do you give me orders? I'm the boss, not you."

Max leans on the table. “Not tonight. Do yourself a favor, Nick, and pull your head out of your ass.” He stands, catches the bartender’s eye and gives him a nod. Max walks out. Jesse and Alex follow.

The waitress brings me over a beer. “Mike says this is the last one and then he’s calling you a cab.”

Grabbing the beer I, down it in one long gulp, and stand up a little too quickly, causing the chair to scrape the floor. After throwing some money on the table I get Mike’s attention. “I’ll be outside.” He nods and picks up the phone.

Stepping outside into the cooler air makes my head spin a little. I take a deep breath then stagger to the corner of the building to wait for the cab.

Suddenly I am pulled backwards into the alley by my shirt collar. My feet give out from under me and I end up on my ass. “What the fuck?” It is too dark to see my attacker. A pair of hands grab the front of my shirt and haul me to my feet. I try to throw a right hook, but the alcohol mixed with surprise throws off my aim and I miss. My attacker gives a low, sinister laugh. I try to hit my assailant again, but am punched with what feels like a sledgehammer. My jaw snaps to the right with such force, my molars slam together. I almost throw up from the pain. The second shot goes straight to my gut, knocking the wind out of me. The hands let go of me and I fall onto my hands and knees. Bits of gravel cut into my palms. I suck in a big gulp of air when someone grabs a fistful of my hair from behind, jerking my head up and back.

A man whispers in my ear, “Don’t hurt her again.”

As quickly as it began, it is over. After a few seconds, I stand ready to throw down, but I am completely alone.

The next day I walk into the kitchen at Mio Angelo’s kitchen to see Gina. She takes one look at my face and rushes over.

“Oh my God, Nick. What happened?”

A huge purple and black bruise runs along my jaw and snakes up my cheek. It is swollen and hurts like a bitch.

"You tell me."

Her brows draw together. "What do you mean?"

Marco walks into the kitchen from the storeroom, takes one look at the expression on my face, and quickly turns around.

"I was at the bar last night. While I was waiting outside for a cab, some guy grabbed me and dragged me into the alley. I got this" —I point to my jaw— "and a message, *Don't hurt her again.*"

She takes a step back from me, her face draining of color. "You think I set you up? Are you insane?"

I cross my arms. "If it wasn't you, maybe it was Ray, or your father, or even dear old Uncle Walt, maybe?"

She flinches as if I struck her. For a second I feel like a total asshole, but I move my jaw and the pain changes all that.

"Nick, I'm sorry you got hurt, but I didn't have anything to do with it, I swear! I never told my family about our fight and haven't even seen Uncle Walter since Abby and Max's wedding."

Walt is Gina's father's best friend. They were Marines together and while Gina's dad got out and went into a legitimate business, Walt went a different route. To the outside world he runs a 'security' firm, but in reality he is a mercenary. This attack isn't really his style, but I am grasping at straws.

"Then who did this to me, Gina, huh? I didn't do it to myself."

There are tears in her eyes, but I don't care. "I think we need to take a break for a while."

She gasps. "WH—what? Why?"

I sigh. "Things just aren't working, Gina. I need to decide if this relationship is worth me getting my face bashed in for."

She looks down and wrings her hands in her lap. "I see."

"Yeah, well, I'm gonna go. I'll call you in a few days."

She never looks at me, just nods.

I walk out.

GINA

Marco comes back into the kitchen with Abby close at his heels. He walks came over and wraps his arms around me. He doesn't say a word. I am grateful for that. Silent tears course down my cheeks and drip into my lap.

Abby squats in front of me. “Sweetie?”

I sniffle. “He wants a break.” Marco’s arms tighten around me.

“For how long? Why?”

I shrug and mumble into Marco’s shoulder, “I don’t know. Someone beat him up behind the bar last night and he thinks I set him up.”

Abby shoots to her feet. “What? What the hell, Gina?” I shrug out of Marco’s embrace and rest my head on his shoulder. In front of me Abby paces the kitchen. She is pissed. When that happens, no one is safe.

"He's got a lot of nerve thinking you would do that to him. What the hell is wrong with that boy? I have half a mind to find him and kick his ass!"

Watching Abby pace the kitchen, ranting like a lunatic makes me smile. She is always ready to throw down for me and always has my back.

"Why are you smiling?" Abby stands in front of me, her fists planted firmly on her hips.

I stand and hug her. "Io amo, te poco cazzuto."

I love you, you little badass.

She hugs me with such ferocity, I almost lose my breath. "Ti amo, anch'io." *I love you, too.*

I give her a squeeze and take a step back. Taking a deep breath, I wipe my eyes. Giving my closest friends a wobbly smile, I clap my hands. "Okay, people, let's get back to work."

We work for a few hours in uncomfortable silence. Tommy starts his shift as dinner service began. As usual he came through the kitchen on his way to the pizzeria.

He takes one look at everyone and knows something is wrong.

“What’s going on with everyone?”

Marco glances at me, but says nothing. Tommy turns to Abby, but she keeps her head down as well.

I sigh. “Nick and I are taking a break.”

Tommy comes over to where I am plating salads for the dinner rush and squeezes my shoulder. “I’m sorry. Are you alright?”

The sincere look in his eyes makes my heart melt a little. “I’m fine, Tommy, but thanks.”

He nods. “Remember, I have those shoulders if you need them.” He kisses the top of my head and smirks as he grabs a cherry tomato off the plate I am working on.

Uncle Ray sticks his head through the pizzeria doors. “Tommy, I’m not paying you to eat the food. Let’s go.”

“Yes, sir.” He gives me a wink and follows Uncle Ray.

Abby watches him go. “What the hell was that?”

I shrug. “He was just being nice.”

Marco and Abby exchange a glance. “What?”

Abby walks over to stir the vodka sauce simmering on the stove. “Just be careful with Tommy, okay? Something about him seems a little off to me.”

I give her a dismissive wave. “It’s fine, but thanks.”

Later that night I go to see my mom and do laundry. She is drying dishes in the kitchen when I walk in.

“Hi, Mom.”

She puts down the pot and pulls me in for a hug. Pulling back, she frowns. “What’s wrong?”

No one can ever put one over on my mom. I swear she can break the toughest man with a single look.

“Nick and I are taking a break.”

“I see.” Mom points for me to sit at the kitchen table. As I sit, she pulls out a bottle of whiskey and two glasses. Two fingers worth of the amber liquid is placed in front of me. Mom sits opposite me, her own glass holding a little less than mine.

“I’m listening.”

I swallow the amber liquid in one gulp and hiss as the burn travels slowly down my throat. I quickly replace the liquid in my glass as my mom sips from hers.

I tell her everything. One of the things I love about my mother, she doesn’t judge and will not give her opinion unless she’s asked.

I didn't realize I started crying until she hands me a napkin. I am drying my eyes when my father walks in.

“Gina? What’s wrong?” He jerks me from my chair and into his arms. He strokes my hair and whispers in Italian.

At times like this, I am a total daddy’s girl.

I give him a squeeze and sit back down.

“Gina and Nick are taking a break.”

“A break? What the hell does that mean?”

Mom rises and takes out a third glass. She pours my father a shot and places it in front of him as he sits to my right.

“Explain to me what *taking a break* means, please.”

Making sure certain details—like Nick’s accusations of my family arranging his assault—stays out of the conversation, I explain what is going on in my relationship. Dad stays silent throughout my explanation. He doesn't need to say a word; the rising color in his cheeks speaks volumes.

“So what are you supposed to do now, sit around and wait for him to make up his mind?”

I shrug. “I don’t know.”

My mother reaches out and grasps my hand. “What does your heart tell you, baby?”

That is the problem. I just don't know.

“I think you should let Abby beat the crap outta him and send him packing! He has a lot of nerve. I mean, who does he think he is? Does he think you’re just going to wait around until he pulls his head out his mommy's ass and grows the hell up?"

A laugh bubbles up from my chest and I can't stop it. That's my father. He usually has no filter and gives you his honest opinion whether you want it or not.

"You know what, Dad? You're right. I doubt he's sitting at home pining over me, so why should I waste one more tear on him?"

Dad raises his glass and salutes me. "Dannatamente ragione, cazzo di lui!"

Damn right, fuck him!

Mom rises and grabs the bottle of whiskey. "You two have had enough. I'm going to bed."

My father winks. I giggle.

NICK

"Ma, seriously, I'm fine." I sigh as she places a towel filled with ice against my face.

She mutters as she walks over to the stove, "Non posso credere che la puttanella ha fatto questo al mio bambino." *I can't believe that little whore did this to my baby boy.*

I sigh again as my father speaks in Gina's defense. "Teresa, stop it. I know Gina. She's a good girl; she wouldn't do this to him."

She *tsks*. "Thugs. That's what they are. The whole family." She turns from the stove and points at me. "You and that girl are done. Do you hear me? Done!"

"Ma, please, huh? My head hurts and I can't deal with you yelling at me right now."

Her eyes soften as she kisses my good cheek. “I’m sorry, sweetie. Why don’t you go lie down and I’ll bring you dinner later?”

I rise from the table and kiss her cheek. “Okay. Thanks, Ma.”

I walk out of the room, but not before I hear my father speak, “Teresa, stop babying him! He’s a man, damn it, and it’s time he acted like one. He can’t do that if you’re always fixing his boo-boos. Besides you and I both know that Gina’s family didn’t do this to Nick. If Ray or Vince thought for one second that your baby boy hurt Gina, they wouldn’t have hurt Nick; they would have killed him”

The spoon slams on the counter. “Shut up, Dominic! I am his mother and I will always take care of him. He needs to find the right girl and that little puttana certainly isn’t the one.”

Dad sighs and shuffles off to the den. I did the same.

GINA

By the end of the week, I am frustrated. Everyone is treating me with kid gloves and I am sick of it. I waited all week to hear from Nick, but he keeps up the silent routine. The pity party needs to stop. Taking matters into my own hands, I make an announcement.

Marco and Abby are in the kitchen when I breeze in Saturday morning. I took extra time to pick out my outfit today and did my hair and make up for the first time in a week. I am done waiting by the phone for Nick Zacco. I want to go have some fun, damn it!

"Tonight after work, we're going dancing."

Abby and Marco stop working. Marco lets out a whoop. "There's my girl."

I give him a kiss on the cheek. "Damn right. I've wallowed long enough. Tonight, I want to go out and have fun. I want to drink way too much and dance all night. Who's with me?"

Marco spins me around before dipping me. "I'm in!"

Abby smiles. "What the hell. Me, too."

I smile. "Good. Let's say nine o'clock at the bar? They have live music tonight."

Marco and Abby agree and we get back to work.

Getting ready actually raises my spirits. I am excited about having a night out with my friends. I choose a red silk sleeveless blouse and pair it with a short black skirt. A pair of red peep-toe pumps complete the outfit. Most women would opt for different shoes for dancing, but I have been wearing heels for so many years, I feel awkward in flats. Well, except for the damn Crocs I wear in the kitchen.

Not that I'll ever admit that to anyone.

I take a cab to the bar and laugh to myself as I walk in thinking about those stupid shoes. Scanning the room for my friends, the smile drops from my lips when I spot them.

Apparently I didn't make myself clear about tonight. I expected to see Marco and Abby. What I *didn't* expect to see is Marco and Abby cuddling up to James and Max.

Seriously?

All couples and me. *Yippee*. I am ready to duck out when Marco spots me. He stands and waves like a madman until James yanks him back down. Plastering on the brightest smile I can muster, I head to the table.

“My, don’t you look pretty?” Marco coos. James nods in agreement. He never speaks much.

Max agrees. “You look good, kiddo. Thanks for inviting us out tonight.”

My fake smile never wavers. “No problem. The more the merrier.”

The waitress drops off a round of drinks. I am grateful to see an extra dirty martini in front of me. I snag her attention.

“We’re also gonna need six tequila shots, please.”

Abby sips on her glass of red wine. “Do you think that’s wise?”

I shrug and take a healthy sip of my martini. The salty taste is perfect. “I don’t care about being wise right now.”

She doesn't respond. When the waitress comes back with our shots, Marco and I are the only ones who opts to drink them. We raise the first shot.

“Here’s to those who wish us well and those who don’t can go to hell!”

Marco giggles as I down the shot. I repeat the process two more times and feel much better.

“Gina, honey, maybe you need to slow down.” Abby looks concerned.

I try to focus on her face, but it is difficult. “You know what, Abby? I think I’m doing just fine considering my boyfriend basically broke up with me and I’m out with a bunch of *couples* tonight.”

She gasps. “I’m sorry, Gina. We didn’t think . . . .” She looks at Marco for help.

I glare. “No you didn’t. You know what? I wanna dance.”

I stand and wobble for a second before recovering my footing. I wind my way onto the crowded dance floor and let the rhythm take over. Closing my eyes, my hips sway back and forth. For the first time in a week, I feel free and happy. When a pair of hands grasp my hips, my eyes fly open.

“I like the way you move.”

I recognize that voice.

I turn to find a grinning Tommy. He holds tight to my hips and pulls my back closer to his chest. He moves in time to the music with ease. I close my eyes again and grind my ass against him.

When the music changes to something slower, Tommy turns me around in his arms, my cheek resting on his chest. I take a deep breath. He smells of cologne and sweat. It is intoxicating; or maybe it is all the tequila coursing through me. I don't care.

I open my eyes. “Kiss me.” Tommy shakes his head. “You’ve had a lot to drink tonight, Gina. I don’t want to take advantage. I’m out here to keep you safe from the guys who’ve been eye-fucking you all night.”

I snort. “Honey, no one was doing that.”

He stops dancing. “Gina, *every* man was doing that. I don’t think you realize just how sexy you are. The way you look tonight, moving the way you do? It’s taking every ounce of self-control I have not to take you to bed and keep you there for a week.”

“Tommy, I . . . .”

He releases me and takes a step back. “I know. Nick still holds your heart and I want to be more than a drunken distraction. You’re worth more than that, Gina, and frankly, so am I.”

Before I can say another word he steps back and fades into the crowd. I feel sick and defeated. It is time to go home. When I get back to the table to get my purse, everyone is quietly staring at me.

“What?”

Abby shakes her head. “What are you doing Gina?”

Pointing to the dance floor, I look Abby in the eye. “That was me being rejected by yet another man. I’m going home.” I grab my purse.

Max grabs my wrist. “We’re just looking out for you, Gina. Let us drive you home.”

Wrenching my arm back, I spit. “I can take care of myself. I’ll get a cab.” I stalk off toward the door.

The cool air hits when I get outside. It prickles my skin—I worked up a light sweat while dancing. I shiver.

“Here.”

A sweatshirt appears out of nowhere and drapes over my shoulders. I turn. Nick stands there with his hands in his pockets.

“What are you doing here?”

“I came looking for you.”

I pull the sweatshirt closer around my shoulders and shiver again.

“Was that Tommy Reynolds dancing with you?”

I nod.

“I didn’t like it.”

I let out an exasperated sigh. “Nick, you were the one who wanted to *take a break*, not me. I sat alone in my apartment night after night for almost a week. I didn’t see or hear from you. I thought we were over. So tonight I just wanted to have some fun with my friends, but they brought their husbands and I felt left out and lonely. So yeah, when Tommy came to dance with me, I didn't stop him. It felt *good* to be wanted by a man."

He looks pained. "You think I don't want you?"

My shoulders slump. "Nick, at this point I don't know what the hell's going on."

He closes the distance between us. His lips crash over mine. He makes a statement with his body that he can't with his words. He backs me up until I hit the wall of the bar. The rough brick exterior scrapes my back as Nick grinds his hardened length into my stomach. Swallowing my moans, his hands snake under my blouse. His deft fingers pull the lacy cup of my bra down and my nipple pebbles. He caresses my breast with his calloused palm before giving the tight nipple a little squeeze. Desire floods throughout my entire body before pooling between my legs. His other hand makes its way under my skirt. As his fingers graze over my panties, I whimper.

He stops and steps back. The unmistakable look of desire is all over his face.

“Gina, as much as I want to fuck you right here and now, I think we need to go to your place where I can take my time and love you the right way.”

I nod. Nick throws me over his shoulder and practically sprints to his truck. We are halfway across the parking lot when Abby and Max come out of the bar. She smiles and waves. I blow her a kiss as Max chuckles, pulling Abby closer to his side.

If I paid closer attention, I would have noticed another person watching Nick and I as well. He didn't smile.

NICK

I didn't expect to go out tonight, but when Max called and told me that Gina was going to be at the bar, I couldn't stay away.

I miss her. I didn't realize how much I loved her until our relationship was put on hold. My mother went into smother overdrive since my assault. She is making it impossible to stay at home anymore. I found an apartment across town and broke the news to my parents over dinner last night.

Dad is ecstatic. Mom is not.

"So now you're going to leave me, too? You're just like Frank. Are you going back to that girl, too?"

I sighed. "Ma, I love you. I'm only going across town, for Christ's sake."

She cuffed my ear. "Don't you cuss in this house, Nick."

"Yes, ma'am. As far as Gina's concerned, yes I'm going to see if she'll take me back."

Mom made a pained sound. She quickly stood from the table, clearing our dishes. She grabbed my father's plate.

He protested, "I wasn't done, Teresa."

She scowled and slammed the plate in front of him. "Here. Aren't you going to say anything about this?"

He resumed eating. "About what?"

Mom threw her hands in the air. "About your son ruining his life for that puttana."

I slammed my hand on the table and stood. "Enough!"

My mother jumped. Her hand flew to her chest.

Dad continued to eat his dinner as if nothing had happened.

"Ma, I don't ever want to hear you refer to the woman I love as a whore ever again. Do I make myself clear?"

She glared. "I—"

I spoke through gritted teeth. "Do. I. Make. Myself. Clear?"

She turned her back to me and grabbed a sponge from the sink. . "Fine."

I knew she wasn't happy, but I couldn't live my life for her anymore. I had to start living for me. Me and Gina.

Dad picked up his wine glass and gave me a salute. "Go get her, son."

I nodded and left.

Now I am in Gina's apartment telling her the whole story. I wipe the tears streaking down her cheeks with my thumb.

"Don't cry, baby."

She gives me a slight smile. "I can't believe you did that for me, for us."

I smile. "I think it's about time I became a grown up, don't you?"

She shifts on the couch until she straddles my waist. "You know, you could always move in here with me."

I am getting hard. This conversation needs to end quickly. "No. I need to prove to myself that I can really do it on my own, but I love you for offering."

She bends to kiss me. "I'm so proud of you."

When her lips finally meet mine, it is like coming home.

The kiss starts out gentle, but quickly morphs into something more. My tongue demands entrance and Gina opens for me. She tastes like tequila and lime. My hard-on strains against my zipper, causing me some pain. I shift. Gina moans.

I love that she is so responsive. My hands tangle in her hair as I rise from the couch. She instinctively wraps her legs around my waist and grinds herself into me. I feel her heat through our clothes. Never breaking the kiss I maneuver us into the bedroom. I gently lay her down on the mattress and slowly unbutton her blouse. Pulling back the material, I suck in a breath. She has on a black lace bra. "Beautiful."

Gina arches her back. I slip the straps down and unclasp the back. She sits up slightly and I toss the garments to the floor. Her skirt is next. She lays on the bed in her black lace panties as I shed my clothes. When I am naked, her eyes roam over me with a hunger in I haven't seen in a long time. She licks her lips. I watch her tongue dart out and follow its movement. I groan. Gina tries to scoot up the bed, but I grab her ankles and pull her back to the edge. “Stay.”

She sits up on her elbows. “Yes, sir.”

I groan and grasp the side of her panties. The lace gives way easily as I rip them from her luscious hips. Gina gasps as my head dips between her legs.

She is so wet, I almost come on the spot. My tongue swipes from ass to clit. Gina writhes on the bed. I place a hand on her taught stomach as if to anchor her before lapping her up like she is my favorite ice cream cone.

“Oh God, Nick. Don’t stop.”

I swirl my tongue around her clit and slip in a finger into her swollen folds. A second finger joins the first and I curl my fingers, hitting her G-spot.

She hisses. “Fuck!”

I pump in and out of her while continuing to assault her clit. My hand moves from her stomach up to her breast and I roll her tight nipple through my fingers.

“Nick, I’m so close.”

Pinching her nipple while gently biting her clit made Gina scream my name.

I reach into the nightstand and grab a condom. After quickly rolling it on, I rejoin Gina on the bed and nuzzle her neck.

She moans and squirms. “Nick, please.”

I rise and thrust into her. I want to take my time, but when she clamps around my cock, I know I can't. Gina arches her back, taking me deeper. Her hands travel over my back, her heels press into my ass, keeping me in place.

"Baby, are you alright? Did I hurt you?"

She opens her eyes. "No. You feel so amazing; I just wanted it to last a little longer."

At this moment, Gina owns me heart and soul.

"I want to go slow with you, but I don't know if I can."

She shifts. "Go slow next time. Right now I need you to fuck me fast and hard, Nick."

I grunt and pick up the pace. Gina reaches up and pulls her nipples. It is so fucking hot. Gina's breathing picks up, she is close. My own orgasm is building at the base of my spine. Reaching down, I rub my thumb over her clit and send her flying. She screams my name. Two thrusts later, I empty into her.

I roll off her. After a minute I go to the bathroom and dispose of the condom. Gina is laying on the bed trying to catch her breath. With her eyes closed and her hair splayed on the pillows, she looks happy and satisfied. I pull the covers back and climb into bed. Gina snuggles to my side and falls asleep. After listening to her breathing for a few minutes, I do the same.

***

I am having the most erotic dream. Gina is giving me the best blowjob of my life. It has to be a dream because blow jobs aren't high on Gina's list of favorite sexual activities.

Her warm tongue glides over my stiff cock. Her soft moans vibrate through me. My hands plunge into her hair as her tempo increases. When her teeth gently scrape up my shaft, I come long and hard.

"Well that wasn't so bad."

My eyes snap open. Gina is on her knees between my legs. Thick pools of cum are on my stomach and a drop is on the corner of her mouth.

"I thought I was dreaming."

She grins. “I thought I’d give it a shot. No pun intended.”

I laugh and look at my stomach. “I guess I missed.”

Gina wrinkles her nose. “You didn’t, but I’m sorry, that’s gross and I’m not swallowing it.”

I laugh. “How would you know? You’ve never swallowed it before.”

She runs a finger over my abs and swirls it in the now congealing mess. “It reminds me of runny rice pudding and that shit’s gross.”

I lay my head back on the pillow and laugh. Gina’s frankness is what I love about her.

“Well, honey, it looks like I need a shower, then.”

She stands and saunters toward the bathroom with an extra sway in her hips. I love it when she puts on a little show for me. When I hear the water running, I join her.

GINA

My head is spinning and it isn't from last night's tequila shots. I can't believe Nick came to the bar to get me. When he told me how he was moving out and then actually stayed the night, I felt happier with our relationship than I had in a very long time.

Giving Nick a blowjob this morning is my way of going out of my comfort zone for him. I still won't swallow his cum. Abby says she didn't like it until she did it with Max and now it's her favorite thing. I shudder; I don't think I'll ever want to swallow that stuff.

The shower curtain draws back. Nick gives me a shy grin. "Room for one more?"

I smile and move to the side so he can get in. I reach for the body wash Nick kept here and lather my hands. We shift positions so Nick can stand under the spray and get the mess off his stomach. When he turns around, water drips off his nose and down his chest toward his sculpted abs. He has the perfect V-shaped body; broad chest and narrow hips that leads down to strong thighs. The dark stubble lining his jaw completes the rugged look. He keeps *all* of his body hair trimmed; a practice I am grateful for this morning.

I turn him around. He tenses then relaxes as my soapy hands massage his back muscles. I work my way up and down his spine. Nick puts his arms on the shower wall for balance as I work my way down to his hard ass. I drop to my knees and rub the backs of his thighs. He turns when I finish and I am faced with his hardened cock. It pulses and jumps under my gaze. I lean forward to take it in my mouth, but Nick has other ideas. He pulls me up and kisses me.

A shiver runs through me. He whispers into my neck, “My turn to wash you.”

Nick adjusts the water temperature so it is a little hotter and grabs my body wash. The scent of apples fills the room as Nick's hands fill with lather and bubbles. He turns me around so my back is pressed against his chest. His hands caress my neck and slowly move down to my breasts. My already puckered nipples tighten at his touch. My legs wobble.

Nick snakes one hand around my waist to hold me up. "I've got you, baby."

His other hand makes its way toward my belly button and below. I spread my legs wider as his fingers reach between my folds. Nick groans. "You feel like heaven." He swirls his thumb around my clit as his fingers stroke my swollen folds. Nick inserts one finger into me and then a second. My body greedily clamps down on his fingers.

Nick chuckles. "Not yet, baby."

I moan as he continues to slowly pump his fingers. When I am about to come, Nick suddenly pulls out.

I whimpers in protest as he spins me around, crushing his lips to mine. "I need to have you now, but I didn't bring a condom in with me."

Even though I have been on the pill for years and Nick and I are both clean, we always use a condom, but right now I didn't want to stop.

"Don't stop, Nick."

He spins me back around and thrusts into me from behind. I use the shower wall to brace myself as Nick pumps into me hard and fast.

"Oh God, yes!"

Nick reaches around and flicks my clit. I scream his name as the orgasm I had been denied a few moments ago tears through me. He shouts my name and I feel hot liquid fill me. We stay that way for a few moments, trying to catch our breath.

"Holy shit." Nick pulls out of me. I instantly miss him.

"That was amazing."

Nick turns me around and gathers me in his arms. His eyes search mine. "Are you alright with what we just did? I know you're on the pill, but it's not always one-hundred percent." I nod and relief passes over his face.

We quickly clean up and get out of the shower.

As we are drying off, I realize it is Sunday morning and Nick missed church with his mother. When I remind him, guilt flashes in his eyes, but quickly disappears.

"She's going to have to start going by herself or with my dad, I guess."

I smile and stroke his face. "Don't shut her out completely, Nick. She loves you."

He turns his head and sighs. "I know, but I need some time away right now to breathe."

"Okay."

"What have you got going on today?"

I pick out a pair of black skinny jeans and a deep purple sweater. Lacy purple underwear complete the outfit. Nick looks like he wanted to rip off my panties again, so I move to the other side of the bed to dress. I like these panties. "It's Sunday. The family will be here at noon to cook dinner together downstairs."

Nick zips up his jeans and grabs his shirt. “Oh, right. I forgot. I’ll guess I’ll go home and start packing, then.”

I zip my jeans and turn to face him. “Do you have to? I thought you’d want to stay for dinner.”

His smile makes my heart melt. “Are you sure?”

I cross the room and hug him around the waist. “Absolutely. Only be prepared, my family’s a little pissed at you right now.”

Nick winces. “I guess they would be, huh?”

I laugh. “Let’s just say it might be easier to deal with your mother today than my father.”

He shrugs. “Maybe, but Abby cooks better than my mother—the reward outweighs the risk.”

Nick ran home to change into clean clothes. I head downstairs to help Abby start dinner. She always came about a half an hour before everyone else to organize the ingredients for the family meal.

She gives me a knowing smirk when I walk into the kitchen and then looks behind me.

"He went home to get clean clothes, you nosey bitch."

Abby chuckles as she pulls out veggies for the salad from the walk-in. Max comes into the kitchen from the dining room. He gives me a smile and looks around the room. "Where's Nick?"

Abby answers for me. Max gives me a hug. "I'm glad you guys worked it out."

I hug him back. "Me, too."

Abby hands me a bowl of lettuce. I take it over to the sink to wash. "So he's coming back to face the firing squad, huh? I don't know if he's brave or stupid, facing us all at once."

I shrug. The water runs over the delicate green leaves. "I think the only ones that are going to give him a problem are Uncle Ray and dad. Everyone else should be fine." I look pointedly at Abby. "Right?"

Abby doesn't say anything for a full minute. Finally, she looks me in the eye, giving me her *don't bullshit me* look. “Are you alright?”

I know what she is asking and nod. “I think so.”

Abby's eyes soften. “Then, yes.”

Max walks over and kisses the top of Abby's head. “Good girl.”

I smile and go back to washing the lettuce.

NICK

I get home and run in and out of my apartment as quickly as possible, hoping to avoid my mother. Instead I run into my father who is taking out the garbage.

"Hey, Dad."

He smirks. "Where were you last night?"

I wince. "Gina's."

He nods, the smile never leaving his face. "Heading back there now?" His eyes drop to the overnight bag in my hand.

"Yeah. We're having dinner with her family. I'll go straight to work from there in the morning."

"Does her father know you'll be there today?"

I shake my head. "No."

My father clasps my shoulder. “Don’t lose your head today. You hurt his only child, his little girl. He’s going to be pissed as hell at you. Ray, too, I expect. Be a man and take it, then apologize and shake his hand. Give him the respect he deserves and you’ll be fine.”

“Thanks, dad.” I turn to walk away.

“Oh, and, Nick?” I turn back. “Don’t freeze your mother out too much longer. I can’t take the hurt away from her, only you can.”

I nod and walk away.

When I get back to Gina’s, the back parking lot is full. I sigh. I want to talk to Gina’s father and uncle first and get everything squared away before dinner.

As luck would have it, both of them walk out the back door and spot me immediately. I get out of my truck and head straight into the lion’s den.

“Mr. Toriello.”

“Nick.”

I nod at Ray, but he silently glares at me.

“I wanted to speak to you about Gina.”

Ray tenses. I try to stay calm.

“Did you now?” Mr. Toriello stands with his arms crossed over his chest.

“Yes, sir. I wanted to apologize to you for the hurt I caused her. I was being a stupid, scared asshole and she didn’t deserve to be treated that way.”

Ray continues to stare me down. Mr. Toriello only nods. A trickle of sweat rolls down my back.

“I want you to know that I love your daughter. I swear that I will never ever hurt her like that again.”

Mr. Toriello looks at Ray. The silent conversation they have with their eyes causes more sweat to roll down my back.

Finally Mr. Toriello looks at me. “Fine.” He turns and goes back into the restaurant.

Ray stays outside a minute longer. “My brother in law is much more forgiving than I. Make no mistake; this was your one free pass. *One. Capisce*?”

I swallow and nod. “Yes, sir.”

He turns and walks back into the restaurant.

I take a deep breath and lean against the side of the building. The back door swings open and Max comes out, a beer in each hand. He looks me over.

“You look alright to me. Thought you might need this.” He hands me the beer. I take a long pull from the bottle.

“Thanks.”

Max nods. “How bad was it?”

“Veiled death threats aside, I think it went well.”

Max claps my shoulder. “Good. C’mon inside. Gina’s waiting for you.”

I smile and swallow the rest of the beer. “Let’s go.”

GINA

I am freaking out. When Nick's truck pulls up and my father and uncle immediately head outside, I panic. I jump to follow them, but am stopped by my mother. "No."

"But, Mom, they're going to kill him."

Carina comes over and rubs my back. "No they won't. They might scare him, but they won't kill him."

Mom smiles. "She's right. You have to understand, honey, your father and uncle are looking out for you. The men in this family are very protective over what they love and they love you very much. Your father and uncle just need Nick to be aware that what he did to you was *not* okay. They want him to know he won't get another chance to hurt you like that again."

I look at the back door. "Are you sure?"

Carina laughs and hands me a glass of wine. "Yes. Let them do their job and if Nick is a smart man, he will let them have their say and apologize. If he does, all will be forgiven."

I expel a breath. "Oh, good."

Carina gives me a pointed look. "I said forgiven, Gina, not forgotten. *Never* forgotten." She smiles and walks away.

I lean in, whispering to my mother, "Does she scare you, too?"

My mother looks over my head. Carina is talking to Max's mother. "Just a little."

I shudder, thinking what a powerful force she and Uncle Ray are together and feel bad for Max.

"Max better keep Abby happy."

Mom chuckles. "Damn right."

Dinner went well. Despite some residual tension between Nick and the men, he is invited outside to have a cigar with them between dinner and dessert.

Nick stays over that night. We make love twice. He is so sweet and gentle; holding me close, whispering declarations of love in my ear until I fall asleep.

The next morning I wake to find I am alone in bed. The sheets are cool, Nick has been gone a while. It is after eight. I can't believe how well I slept. I smile, touching my lips, remembering the previous night's lovemaking. I roll over and stretch. My body is sore in the most delicious way. I pick up Nick's shirt from last night and pull it over my head. I inhale his scent—a combination of musk and his favorite cologne—and smile. When I get to the kitchen, I stop short. Nick made himself at home like the last time, but unlike the last time, the kitchen is spotless. There is a note next to the coffeepot.

Gina,

You looked so beautiful sleeping that I didn't have the heart to wake you. I wanted to, believe me, but there's plenty of time for that tonight.

Thank you for giving me a second chance. I know I don't deserve it or you, but I will spend the rest of my life making up for the pain I've caused you.

All my love,

Nick

A single tear slides from my eye as I reread the note. A smile slips over my face. I want to surprise Nick. Maybe I'll show up at the job site in lingerie and a trench coat? No, the guys will never let me live that down. Flowers are too girly and balloons too juvenile. Finally the idea hits me. I quickly grab the phone and dial.

"Good morning. Zacco Construction, how may I help you?"

“Edward, its Gina.”

“Gina! How are you?”

“Great. How’s the job going?”

Edward chuckles. “As long as I bring in banana nut muffins every Monday, it’s fine.”

I giggle. “Just watch him with those. His cholesterol isn’t so hot.”

Edward whispers, “Promise to keep a secret?”

“Sure.”

“The recipe is actually heart healthy. After Ray had his heart attack, Jessica’s mother started watching her husband’s diet. Together she and Jessica reworked the recipe. So far no one’s complained.”

I laugh. “That’s great. Listen, I want to bring Nick lunch today, but I don’t know where he’s working. Can you help me out?”

There is some clicking in the background then Edward says, “The crew is over on Maple doing some roof work for the Hartley’s.”

A smile spreads over my face. “Thanks so much, Edward.”

“Anytime, Gina.”

I showered and dressed. There is enough time for me to whip something up and bring it to Nick by lunchtime.

The restaurant is closed on Mondays. Uncle Ray is getting the dough out of the walk in fridge when I make my way into the kitchen.

“Good morning, Bella. What can I do for you?”

I smile and kiss his cheeks. “Nothing, Uncle Ray. I want to fix lunch for Nick and surprise him at work.”

Uncle Ray is shocked. “You came into the kitchen to cook something on your own?”

I laugh. “Cook is a strong word. I’m going to make sandwiches and salad. It’s not really cooking.”

“It’s a start. Tell me, Bella, are you happy? Nick has apologized and you are good?”

I hug him tightly. “Yes, Uncle Ray. I really am. He’s changed for the better.”

He picks up the dough and nods. “Let’s hope so.”

I shake my head and laugh as he heads into the pizzeria to get ready for his day. Wrapped up in thoughts of last night, I jump when someone clears their throat.

“Hungry this morning?”

I spin around. Tommy stands about a foot away, a scowl on his face.

“Tommy! You scared the crap out of me.” He doesn't smile, just stands, staring at the prep table. “No, I’m making lunch for Nick.”

He shifts his feet, staring at me. “I see.”

“Listen, Tommy, about Saturday night.”

Tommy holds up his hand. “It's fine, I get it. Nick is the one you want. It sucks and it hurts. I know that as long as he’s around, I don’t have a shot.”

My chest tightens a little bit. “I’m sorry if I led you on. Really, Tommy, you’re a good guy.”

He sneers. “Not as good as Nick, apparently.”

I am shocked. I have never seen this side of Tommy before. “Tommy, are you going to be alright?”

Tommy brushes past me toward the pizzeria without saying another word.

I finish prepping Nick’s lunch and pack it in take-out boxes from the restaurant. As much as the encounter with Tommy bothers me, I will not let it spoil my day.

I arrive at the jobsite a few minutes before noon. Most of the guys are cleaning up for lunch when I arrive. Max smiles as he walks over to me.

“Hey, pretty lady. What’s up?”

I hold up the cooler bag. “I made Nick lunch.”

Max’s eyebrows shoot up. “Really? You cooked?”

I roll my eyes. “You know, I *can* cook. I prefer it when Abby or someone else does, but I can do it. And no, I didn’t cook. I made sandwiches.”

Max chuckles. “At least you tried.”

I punch him in the arm. “Whatever. Where’s the boss-man, anyway?”

Max points to the roof. “He’ll be right down. Jesse said the air nailer was acting funny so Nick went up to take a look at it.” He turns and whistles at Nick.

Nick’s face lights up when he sees me. “Hey, babe. What’s up?”

I wave and shake the bag. “I made you lunch.”

“Really? I’ll be down in a second; I need to check this out first.” He waves the nail gun in his hand.

“Jesus, Nick! Don’t wave that thing around. Be careful.”

He laughs. “Don’t worry, babe. Everything’s fine.”

I shudder. “Those damn things make me nervous.”

I watch as Nick tries the air nailer on the roof. It didn't do what it is supposed to. He hits it with his free hand.

Everything happens in slow motion. Nick hits the nail gun with his left hand and it breaks apart as it discharges. Several nails fly back, hitting Nick in the chest and face. One catches him in the neck and a spray of blood erupts just before he falls backwards off the roof.

Max and I charge toward where Nick fell. I make it halfway there when Alex scoops me up and refuses to let me get closer.

“Let me go! Nick!” I shriek and kick Alex; he grunts, but refuses to let me go.

“Gina, no.”

Someone must have called 911. An ambulance roars up the driveway. The paramedics jump out of the rig, racing toward Max. He stands and lets them assess Nick. Max turns to look at me. The look on his face says it all.

Nick is dead.

Somewhere someone screams. It takes a minute before I realize that someone is me. A moment later, my world goes black.

***

Ten days. It'd been ten days since Nick died and I died right along with him. I know my family's worried about me, but I don't care about that now. I don't care about anything.

The whole town came out for Nick's funeral. I remember bits and pieces of it. Jesse crying that it should have been him and not Nick who died. People speaking in whispered tones around me; offering sad smiles and heartfelt words.

I remember Nick's mother wailing when they lowered his casket into the ground. Frank and his wife never left her side. Edward said something about Mr. Zacco selling the business to Max. Mr. and Mrs. Zacco decided to move to Florida to be with Frank and his family.

I want to run away, too, but that requires actually getting out of bed.

I wince as sunlight streams across my face.

“Close the curtains, please.”

My mother stops by every day. She checks on me and forces some soup down my throat before telling me she loved me and going home.

“No. You stink, Gina, and it’s time you got out of that bed.”

I open one eye. Abby walks around my room, picking up crusty tissues and throwing them away.

“Go away, Abby. I’m sick.”

She sighs and sits on the edge of my bed. “I know, sweetie. We’re all very sad that Nick is gone, but you have to get up and come back to us. Please, Gina. Your parents are so worried about you; we all are. Uncle Ray was ready to send Carina up here, but I volunteered instead.”

I shudder. “She scares me.”

Abby giggles. “Me, too. Please, sweetie, get up and take a shower. I’m not saying you have to leave the apartment, just the bed.”

I sigh. “Alright.” I swing my legs over the edge of the bed and stand. Suddenly dizzy, I grab the headboard to steady myself. “Damn it.”

Abby is at my side in an instant. “You’re dehydrated. Wait here.” She runs into the bathroom, returning a second later. “Drink this.” She presses a glass of water into my hand and places a steadying hand on my back. I swallow the cold liquid, my head feels less fuzzy.

“Thanks.”

Abby takes the glass and leads me to the shower. She adjusts the water and helps me undress. When I am in the shower, Abby leaves the bathroom. She leaves out my fluffiest towel. My favorite robe hangs on the back of the door.

I stay in the shower until the water chills. Drying myself off, I notice angles where curves used to be. Nick will have a fit if he sees me like this. He loves my curves.

Nick.

I sank to the floor and cried. After a few minutes, I stand and wash my face. I slip on my robe and head into my bedroom.

Abby had changed the sheets and laid out some clothes for me. I smile at the frilly underwear. Abby really did know me well. Slipping on the black lace, I feel almost back to normal. I slide into the yoga pants and pull the black t-shirt over my head. I brush out my hair and put on my favorite fuzzy slippers. My stomach rumbles at the smell of coffee and bacon.

I pad out to the living room and freeze. Abby set the table for us. It looks beautiful. She put out the good plates, even cloth napkins.

“Abby, it looks and smells amazing in here.”

She comes in carrying a platter of food that can feed a small army. There is bacon, eggs, toast, scones, and yogurt with fresh fruit.

“I wasn’t sure what you wanted or what your system could handle so I made a little bit of everything.” She shrugs, placing the platter in the middle of the table. “Do you want juice, coffee, or both?”

I sit, inhaling deeply. “I think water would be good right now.”

Abby heads back into the kitchen. When she comes out with a pitcher of ice water, she smirks at my heaping plate of food.

“I’m sorry. It smelled too good,” I say around a mouthful of eggs.

Abby fills my water glass. “I’m glad you’re eating again, but slow down before you get sick.”

She is right. I stop and sip my water. “Thanks, Abby.” I give her a lopsided grin.

She sits and helps herself to a scone. “I’m just glad you’re smiling again. You scared us all pretty badly. Your father’s been out of his mind with worry.”

I sigh. “I know. I’ll call him later. What’s been going on in the outside world?”

Abby sips her coffee and shrugs. “Not much. Max took over the construction company and made Alex the new foreman. Edward has been great bringing Max up to speed on the business end of thinks. Together they are making some small changes.”

I nod as I nibble some toast. “Good, that’s good. I’m glad Max took over the company. He’s got a good crew of guys. I’m surprised Jesse stuck around.”

“He’s been working like a madman, says he owes it to Nick to make the company more successful than before. Max is keeping an eye on him and got him to talk to a counselor.”

I pick at a piece of toast. “That’s good.”

Abby changes the subject. “Marco’s been asking for updates about you every day. Maybe you could go downstairs later and see him?”

I sit for a minute. Being so wrapped up in my own grief, I shut out the people who mean the most to me. Deciding it is time to big girl and face the world, I shrug. “Yeah. I could use a dose of Marco.”

Abby reaches for my hand. “Honey, no one’s forcing you back to work if you’re not ready.”

Giving her hand a squeeze, I sigh. “I know, but it’s time I come out of seclusion. Can I just work in the kitchen for now? I can handle you guys, but I’m not ready for the public just yet.” I push my plate away.

Abby stands, clearing the dishes. “You do whatever makes you comfortable. If it gets to be too much, just let me know and we’ll talk.”

I really do have an amazing family.

Two hours later, I am in the kitchen getting the life squeezed out of me by Marco and his boyfriend James.

"Oh, honey. You had us so worried! Don't do that to us ever again." Marco holds onto me, speaking into my ear. "I mean the pissed off girl I can handle but zombie girl? Oh no, we do not like her and *never* want to see her again, okay?"

"Baby, let her breathe." James extracts me from Marco's death grip and places his hands on my shoulders. He isn't wearing his signature shades. "You need anything, baby girl; you let us know, alright?"

He doesn't smile, but the sincerity in his voice makes me tear up. "I promise, James. Thanks."

He gives my shoulders a small squeeze and clears his throat. "I've gotta go." He kisses Marco, puts his shades on, and is out the door moments later.

Marco watches him leave. "He really likes you, honey. He was so worried about you."

"Thanks, Marco."

I grab an apron and ties it around my waist. "Okay, what do you need me to do first?"

Everyone from the family came to see me that night. My father kisses my cheek and holds me for a long time. My mother complains I lost too much weight. Uncle Ray makes me eat two bowls of Minestrone soup to keep his sister happy. The love pouring out of my family is unconditional. I feel terrible for making them worry.

"I'm sorry I upset all of you so much."

My mother waves off my comment with the flick of her wrist. "Baby, you lost the man you loved. We would be more worried if you didn't get lost for a while."

I smile. She always knows what to say to make me feel better.

Later, Tommy comes into the kitchen. The shock on his face is quickly replaced with a smile.

"Hey, Gina. Good to have you back."

"Thanks, Tommy. Good to be back."

He comes over to my station and captures my hands in his. “Remember, I’m here if you ever need *anything*.” He winks, picks up an order from Marco, and walks out the back door.

Abby comes over, her mouth hanging open. “Oh my God, did he just hit on you?”

Marco is as horrified as Abby. “Uh-huh.”

I shudder. “That was a little weird, right?”

Abby walks back to the stove. “Just keep an eye on him, okay? We’ll all keep an eye on him.” She glances at Marco, who is vehemently nodding in agreement. “If he makes you uncomfortable in any way, I’ll have Uncle Ray fire him on the spot. If he touches you, let me know and I’ll kick his ass.”

I nod, too dumbfound to speak.

***

Two days later, the phone calls begin. I answer the phone and no one is there. It happens at all hours, day and night.

My parents want me to move back home, but I am not about to do that over some stupid phone calls, even if they do scare me a little. Instead, I start screening my calls. The hang-ups stop.

The first note is on my car. I am taking out the trash when I notice a piece of paper flapping under my windshield wiper. I think it's junk until I flip it open.

I will never share you with anyone else again.

My eyes snap up. I scan the parking lot; it is empty. My heart races and my hands shake. I run back into the kitchen.

“Gina? Honey, what is it?” Abby rushes over and leads me to a stool. “You’re white as a sheet.”

I can't breathe, my chest constricts like I am having a heart attack. With a shaking hand, I hold out the note. Dizzy, I put my head between my knees and try to breathe.

“What the hell is this?” Abby hands the note to Marco.

“Where was this, Gina?” The concern in Marco’s voice scares me a little more.

I stand to leave, but my heart is still racing and the room begins to spin. “M—my c—car.”

That is the last thing I remember before the darkness overtakes me.

***

Voices. Murmurs all around me, but none are clear. What is that beeping? I try to open my eyes, but they feel like someone glued them shut.

I must have moved because someone touches my cheek.

“Gina? Can you open your eyes for me?”

It is a voice I don't recognize. Where am I? I want to open my eyes, but the darkness pulls me back under.

“She’s been unconscious for two days! Why won’t she wake up?”

“Mr. Toriello, Gina sustained a serious contusion when her head hit the floor. Her body is healing, but I can’t tell you when she will regain consciousness.”

“I’m awake.” I croak, opening my eyes as my father rushes to my side.

“Oh mio dio, bambino. Non hai mai ci scre come quello nuovo!” *Oh my god, baby. Don't you ever scare us like that again!*

He holds me in a bone crushing embrace.

“Dad. Can’t breathe.” I sputter and he lets go.

“Are you alright?”

His eyes search mine.

“My head hurts, but I’m okay.”

A portly man with a really bad comb over stands on the other side of my bed.

“Miss Toriello, I’m Dr. Jensen. Do you remember what happened to you?”

I begin to tremble and my father glares at the doctor. "She just woke up. Do you have to do this now?"

I grab my father's hand and give it a squeeze. "Where's mom?"

As if shaken from a trance, dad looks at me and immediately stands. "Everyone is in the waiting room. They would only let one of us in here at a time. I'll go get her."

As soon as he is out the door, the doctor checks my vitals.

"Oh my God, Gina!" My mother flies through the door. After grabbing me in a hug similar to my father's, she checks me over. "How do you feel?"

I shift in bed and wince. "My head hurts."

Mom glares at the doctor. "Why is my daughter in pain? You assured us that she would be fine!"

Dr. Jensen clears his throat. "A slight headache is normal. I checked her vitals and Miss Toriello seems fine. I'd like her to stay one more night for observation now that she's awake. If all goes well, she can go home tomorrow."

My mother nods. "And her pain?"

Dr. Jensen scribbles something on my chart. "I will have the nurse bring her something for the pain." He smiles at Mom.

She scowls and plants her hands on her hips. "Now would be good."

Dr. Jensen reddens and scurries out of the room.

I giggle and wince as pain shoots through my head. A few minutes later, an older woman with dark brown hair and a warm smile comes in with a glass of water and two white pills. "I hear you're in some pain, sweetie."

I nod and swallow the pills.

"My name's Gloria and I'll be your night nurse. I gave you the extra strength stuff so you should be feeling better soon. Dinner's over, but I can get you something from the cafeteria if you're hungry?"

My stomach grumbles at the mere mention of food. Gloria laughs as she pats my arm. “I’ll take that as a yes. I’ll be right back.” She straightens out my bed covers before heading out the door.

Mom smiles. “I like her.”

When Gloria comes back fifteen minutes later with a grilled cheese sandwich and a bowl of chicken noodle soup, I like her too.

After eating dinner and assuring my entire family that I am alright, they reluctantly go home. The pain meds kick in and I quickly fall asleep.

The next day is utter chaos.

It starts with my parents demanding my release as soon as they walk into the room. Then there is the argument as to where I will stay once I am discharged. My parents want me to stay with them, but I want to go home.

“No.” Dad stands at the foot of my bed and crosses his arms over his chest, jaw set in a hard line.

I sigh while sitting on the edge of the bed waiting for my release papers. My day nurse, Cindy, is young and not very organized; she is currently hunting down my doctor to sign my paperwork. I miss Gloria.

"Dad, I just want to go home, take a long hot bath, and go to bed."

"You can do all those things at our house, Gina." My father is adamant. I look to mom for help, but she is quietly packing my clothes. Her silence means she agrees with my dad.

"Dad, please . . . ."

Cindy bustles into the room with my release papers. "Okey-dokie, here ya go." She goes over my pain management plan then sails out of the room.

"Vince, why don't you go get the car while I speak to Gina."

Dad stops staring at me and glances at Mom. His eyes soften for a moment before he resets his jaw and points at me. “Listen to your mother.” He gives my mother a quick kiss and is gone.

Mom sits down next to me on the bed. She watches my father leave the room. “You scared him. The only other time he was that scared was the day you were born. There were complications and we almost lost you. Two days ago was the first time I ever saw your father cry.”

Dad cries?

My mother gives my hand a gentle squeeze. “You need to understand, you are that man’s world. Even I come in second to you.”

I open my mouth to protest, but she smiles and shakes her head. “It’s the way it’s supposed to be. Your father and I would lay down our lives for you. When he thought you weren’t going to wake up, I heard him pray for God to take him instead.”

Silent tears course down my cheeks.

Mom gently wipes away my tears. "Please come home with us today. Your father needs to protect you. He's very fragile right now. He'll never admit it, but he is."

I wipe the rest of my tears away with the back of my hand. "I need to go home and get a few things first."

Mom smiles as she stands. "That's fine."

My dad had parked right up front. A look of panic crosses his face when he sees me in the wheelchair. He practically jumps over the hood of the car to get to me.

"Are you alright? Why are you in a wheelchair?"

The orderly stops wheeling me and I rush into my father's arms, squeezing him with all my might. "I'm okay, daddy. I promise. The wheelchair is hospital policy, that's all."

He relaxes for a brief moment. He holds on to me as if afraid to let go.

"I'm sorry I scared you, daddy." The tears are back. My father kisses the crown of my head then pulls back. He looks older for a moment, but then he smiles and wipes my tears away with his calloused thumbs. I know things will be better.

I am wrong.

Dad pulls into the parking lot behind the restaurant and turns off the car.

"Dad, I'm just going to run in and grab a few things then I'll be back."

He gets out of the car and opens my door. "I know."

"You don't need to come with me."

He walks ahead of me and opens the door to my apartment with my keys. "I know." He precedes me up the stairs and makes me wait in the hall while he checks out the apartment.

When I get the all clear, I go straight into my bedroom and open my closet to grab some clean clothes and shoes. I remember to pack my Crocs—I fully intend to go back to work tomorrow. Besides, I love those ugly shoes.

The last thing I need is underwear. I open the top dresser drawer and scream. My father tears into my room, screaming my name. When he gets to me, I am on the bed in the fetal position, shaking. He is at my side in an instant.

"Baby, are you alright?"

I point to the dresser.

My father slowly gets up and walks over. He curses.

All my underwear is gone. In the drawer is a red negligee I've never seen before with a note on top:

You will be wearing this when I make you mine.

My father calls out the window to my mother before picking me up in his arms. He carries me to the living room with ease and gently lays me on the couch. Mom flies through the door. "What happened?"

He nods to my bedroom. “Grab her suitcase, but touch nothing else.”

She nods and walks into my room; when she returns a few seconds later with my suitcase, she is pale.

“Vince?” Her voice trembles.

Dad walks into the kitchen and comes out a minute later with my bottle of Jack Daniels and two glasses. He sits them down and pours Mom and me each a healthy portion from the bottle. Taking his phone off his hip, he hits two buttons before holding it to his ear. “Hey, Sarge. It’s Vince. I need a favor.” He tells Walt where we are and hangs up.

Walter Scott is my father’s oldest friend in the world. He and dad were in the Marines together. Even though Walter was higher ranked than my dad, they became best friends. Walter is a trained martial artist; he became fascinated with Isshinryu Karate while their platoon was stationed in Okinawa. My dad studied it for a little while, but he prefers street fighting. Walter, on the other hand, became an eighth degree black belt. He trained my cousin Abby when she came to live with Uncle Ray. Abby recently promoted to third degree black belt status.

When Dad got out of the Marines, he opened his own garage. Walter didn't want the nine-to-five kind of life; he opened up his own business as well. He tells people he runs a security business, but really he and his employees are more than that. No one's ever come right out and said the word *mercenary,* but we've had our suspicions.

I sip from the glass mom pushes into my hand and wince as the burning makes its way down my throat. Remembering I am on pain medication and want to keep my wits about me, I push the glass away and stand.

My fear is replaced by anger. I am pissed that this sicko thinks it is alright to come into *my* home and pull a stunt like this. Not realizing I began to pace to room, I am closest to the door when a heavy knock makes me halt in my tracks. I fling open the door, ready to punch someone.

Walter takes up the entire doorway. He stands at impressive six-foot five-inches tall. His muscular frame hasn't changed much in his fifty-something years—with his line of work, he has to stay in shape.

His hard eyes soften for a moment when he sees me. He scoops me up in a hug.

“Don’t ever just open the door like that, Gina. What if I was the bad guy?” He sits me down and walks past me to shake my father’s hand.

I am about to close the door when someone clears their throat. Startled, I jump back. “Who the hell are you?”

Walt chuckles. “It’s fine, Gina. That’s one of my associates. Cole, meet Gina Toriello.” Cole’s eyes rake over me with a slight frown. Walter calls to Cole. “Come in and meet the rest of the Toriello’s.”

I step aside to allow Cole in. He isn't as big as Walter, but he is no slouch. Cole has to be an inch or so shorter than Walter. He isn't as broad chested either, but he is built like a brick wall. What strikes me the most is what he’s wearing. While Walter is dressed casually in a pair of jeans and a black t-shirt, Cole is the exact opposite in a dark gray Armani suit. The white dress shirt is open at his throat. His Italian loafers gleam with an inky shine. I recognize the designer and they cost more than I make in a month. His light brown hair is short and tousled, like he recently ran his hand through it. The five o'clock shadow running along his strong jaw adds a rugged contrast to his pressed attire. When he looks at me, I almost melt. He has the most piercing blue eyes I have ever seen. Cole gives me a nod and joins everyone in the living room.

I close the door and look at my mother. She looks at Cole for a brief moment and I swear she does a quick sign of the cross over her chest.

Everyone sits on the couches, except Cole. He grabs a chair from the dining table and sits facing us. He crosses his right foot, resting his ankle on top of his left knee. His suit jacket shifts with the movement, revealing his holster and impressive gun.

"Is that a Sig Sauer P226r nine millimeter?"

Cole's eyes snap to mine as he shifts again, trying to conceal his weapon. "It is."

Holy mother of God, his voice can melt butter.

"Can I see it?"

An annoyed look flashes in his eyes. He snorts. "No."

I scowl. "Why not?"

I arch an eyebrow at my parents and Walter, who all seem amused but stay out of the conversation.

"Because I don't want you to hurt yourself, sweetheart."

Oh. No. He. Didn't.

"Oh, really? You don't want me to hurt myself with your big bad gun?" I stand and walk to the hall closet. Pushing back the hangers, I remove the panel, revealing a small wall safe. After entering the code, I open the door and pullout my own Sig Sauer P220 model. I had some modifications done to it—it is the only one of its kind.

“Then you can’t play with mine.” I smile smugly as Cole’s mouth drops open. He stands, coming over to the safe.

“That’s quite an arsenal you have there.”

I shrug. There aren't that many guns. In addition to the Sig, I have a Ruger LC9, and my baby. My baby is a Smith & Wesson military/police model 9mm carry weapon with a full range kit. Seventeen rounds in a clip and I have three additional clips in the safe.

I put the Sig back in its foam form and pick up my baby. I hold it and sigh before putting it back.

I close the safe, smiling at Cole. “Can I see your gun now?”

He smiles, making my heart skip a beat. “Nope.”

I glare at him as he goes back to his chair. I look between Walter, who is trying hard not to smile and my father, who glares at Cole.

“Be careful, Cole. She’s an expert marksman.”

No one outside the immediate family besides Walter knows that, not even Nick.

He snorts again. “I’m sure she thinks she is.”

I reclaim my seat on the couch. “Name the time and place, buddy, and I’ll kick your ass.”

Before Cole answers, Walter holds up his hands. “Alright, let’s not get into a pissing match. Tell me why we’re here.”

My parents and I recount the events of the last few days. The amusement fades from Walter’s eyes as he stiffens in his chair.

He gets up and goes into the bedroom. Cole follows a few seconds later.

My parents and I sit for a few minutes in silence. We listen to Cole and Walter moving around my room. Never having much patience, I get off the couch to see what is going on.

“According to the stuff in her closet, it’s her size.” Cole holds up a dress.

“The note was printed from a computer, not handwritten.” Walter holds the note in a gloved hand.

“No forced entry at the window or the front door.”

“What about the lock?”

Cole shakes his head. “No pick marks. He had a key.”

“A key?”

Both men whip around and stare at me. Walter speaks first. “How long have you been standing there?”

“Long enough. What do you mean he had a key?”

Cole sighs. “There were no marks around the door or the lock so the guy has a key.”

“So this might not have been the first time he was here?”

Walter points to the open drawer. “Since the lingerie is your exact size? Probably not. Who has a key to the apartment, Gina?”

I think for a moment. “Me, Abby, my parents, and Uncle Ray.”

Walter looks around the room. "What about Nick?"

I shake my head. "No. He had a key for the door downstairs, but not the apartment. If I knew he was coming, I would leave the door unlocked."

Cole frowns. "Weren't you guys together for a while?"

I put my hands on my hips. "So?"

He shrugs. "Just seems odd to me, that's all."

I huff. "Not that it's *any* of your business, but Nick never got a key because I didn't want him coming here uninvited. Yeah we were together a while, but there are times when I like to be alone and I couldn't do that if Nick could come and go as he pleased."

Cole smirks. "Not into clingy. Got it."

God, he is infuriating.

I turn to Walter. "Why exactly is he here?"

Walter grimaces. "Cole is going to be handling this for me. I have to go to Europe for a job."

"What? When?"

Walter sighs. “In about three hours.”

I glance over my shoulder at Cole, who regards me with a smirk. “Are you kidding me? Walter, if you seriously think that this stuffy, arrogant son of a bitch is going to be working with me to catch this guy, you are sadly mistaken!”

Cole chuckles. “Work with me? Babe as long as you do as you’re told and stay out of my way, then *I* can catch this guy.”

“*Agh*!” I stomp out of the room, heading straight to the man I know will stick up for me: my daddy.

“Dad, did you know that Cole was going to be in charge of this operation?”

When he averts his gaze and sighs, I get my answer.

“No way, Dad. Not doing it.”

My father stands. “Oh yes you will. Cole is the best in the business next to Walt. Do you honestly think Walt or I would trust your safety, your *life,* to someone who wasn’t the best?”

I huff and drop on the couch in defeat. “No.” I sulked.

My mother rubs my back. “It’ll be fine, baby. You’ll see.”

COLE

Damn that girl is feisty!

When she whips open the door, the look on her face was fierce and determined. I expect a crying mess. Her eyes tell me she cried recently, but the girl Walt and I are dealing with now is in control.

Damn if that doesn't turn me the fuck on.

When she opens her gun safe and caresses the Smith and Wesson, my dick hardens. I walk away and sit back down before I embarrass myself.

I've never had such an immediate reaction to a woman before. The fact that Gina Toriello is smoking hot doesn't help the situation, either. All curves and that hair? An image of bending her over the arm of the couch and wrapping my hands through her hair makes me shift my stance.

Luckily for me, Walt is looking around and doesn't notice my reaction to the woman he considers family.

“I trust you to take care of the daughter of the only man I ever considered to be a brother, Cole. Don’t fuck it up.”

It's the same lecture I got in the car on the way over to Gina’s apartment.

I was with Walt when the call came in. I've never seen him move so fast. He called his pilot and delayed our departure a few hours. That’s when I knew he was serious. Walt and I were heading across the pond to work with his friend who recently left MI6 in Great Britain. Walt wanted to open a second office in London and we were going over there for a few weeks to set it up.

After Walt got the call from Vince Toriello, plans changed—Walt is going to London and I am stuck babysitting.

At first I am pissed about the assignment, but after meeting Gina, I am happy she has a stalker.

That sounds wrong, but I grin to myself anyway.

"So what do you think?"

I am shaken out of my daydreams by Walt. He looks around Gina's bedroom and scowls. "The security here's shit. We need to get a team in here and set up surveillance ASAP."

I agree. "Her father wants her to stay with them, I take it?"

Walter grins. "Noticed the suitcase, too, huh? Probably, but that can't happen."

I put my hands in my pockets. "I guess it's a good thing my bag's in the car, then huh?" Inside, I did a fist pump at the idea of staying here with Gina, but outside I am cool and calm.

Walt narrows his eyes. "This is an operation, Cole. She is a client. Scratch that, she is family and as such you will keep your hands off. If I think for one minute that you've compromised her safety because you were thinking with your dick, I will cut it off. Got it?" The last part comes out a snarl.

I swallow. I have worked for Walt for almost seven years and even though I am loyal, trustworthy, and have risen in the organization, I know the threat isn't an idle one.

"Got it."

Walt nods, pulls out his phone, barks some orders, and hangs up. "Okay, let's go face the firing squad."

I follow Walt into the living room, trying very hard not to smile. Gina is sitting on the couch, glaring at her father. Mrs. Toriello is in the kitchen, because I smell coffee. A second later, my suspicions are confirmed as she comes out of the kitchen carrying a tray loaded with a carafe of coffee, milk, sugar, spoons, cups, and a plate of biscotti. I immediately cross the room, take the tray from her, and place it on the coffee table, which earns me a smile from the women and a scowl from Mr. Toriello.

As Mrs. Toriello pours cups of coffee and hands them out, Walt assesses the situation.

“It looks like our guy has a key to this place. No windows or doors were compromised. He didn’t disturb anything, which means he’s focused. He’s obviously obsessed with Gina and somehow thinks she belongs to him.”

Walt looks to me and I continue, “We think he’s a white male somewhere in his late twenties to early thirties. He was able to secure his own key without anyone noticing and has been able to slip in and out of your apartment unnoticed. That would suggest that he is a familiar face around town.”

Gina pales. “You mean he knows me?”

I nod. “Most likely. Has anyone been paying special attention to you lately? Anyone new or old?”

She sits and thinks for a moment. “No. Well . . . .”

Her father stiffens. “Gina?”

Gina looks me in the eye. “My uncle hired a new delivery guy a few weeks ago, Tommy Reynolds. We went to high school together, but I hadn’t seen him in a while because he was in the military. He got back from his tour a few months ago.”

Walt takes a step closer to Gina. “He’s back for good?”

She nods. “Yes. He and his unit were attacked. He has some pretty nasty scars and said he can’t go back.”

Walt presses. “What about his unit?”

Gina bites her thumbnail. “He never really said, but I got the impression he lost a lot of them.”

I swear. Mrs. Toriello looks nervous. “Should I call Ray and have Tommy fired?” She reaches for her purse.

Walt holds up a hand. “Not yet. I want Cole to observe this guy, first. It could be that he’s just trying to win her affections”

Gina looks visibly pale. I squat in front of her and grab her hands. “Gina, what is it?”

She looks up at me, her eyes glassy. “Nick’s dead because of me, isn’t he?”

Mrs. Toriello gasps. “Honey, no!”

Gina shakes her head. “He is. Nick and I had a terrible fight before he died and someone attacked him in the bar behind the alley. The guy told Nick not to hurt me anymore. Then we made up and the next day his air-nailer malfunctions and he’s dead. It’s my fault.”

“Sweetie, you didn’t cause this. This man is sick and that’s not your fault.” Mrs. Toriello assures her as she rubs Gina's back while I hold her hands.

“Thanks, Mom.”

In that moment, I want to scoop her in my arms and never let go, but first I want to find this guy and show him my Sig up close.

Mr. Toriello stands. “I’m glad you’re staying with us now that we know this guy has a key.”

Walt scrubs the back of his neck and sighs. “Vince, about that . . . .” Walt lays out the plan.

Gina gets up and paces the room. "Walter, I'm not staying here with him."

I love the fact that Gina calls Walt "Walter." I know for a fact that he hates his full name and even see him correct some of the most important people in the world when they mistakenly use it. Gina, however, is able to say it and Walt doesn't even flinch.

"I agree." Mr. Toriello stands and places Gina behind him.

Mrs. Toriello sighs from her place on the couch. She glares at her husband and daughter. "Can we please let Walt finish before we say no?" Father and daughter begrudgingly sit.

I like Mrs. Toriello. She seems to be the voice of reason.

Walt gives Mrs. Toriello a slight nod, sits on the couch, and continues. "We want to draw this guy out. We can't do that if Gina's at your house. We don't want to give him time to get more creative with his stunts and we want this over as quickly as possible, right?"

Heads nod around the room.

"Good. I have a team on their way over to set up surveillance and change the locks. The only ones who will have a key to the new lock are Gina and Cole."

Mr. Toriello protests, but his wife squeezes his thigh, shutting him up.

I really like Mrs. Toriello.

"Okay, Walt. Now how do we explain Cole being here?"

Walt looks at Mrs. Toriello and smile. "How well do the people in town know your side of the family?"

She shrugs. "Some of the older people knew them better, but most of them are dead. Why?"

Walt smiles. "Because Cole is now your nephew."

"What?" All of us ask in unison.

Walt sits back and smiles. "Yup."

After the last of the plan is laid out and everyone is in agreement, Ray, Carina, Max, and Abby are invited to the apartment and brought up to speed.

I like the fact that Gina's family closes ranks around her when they enter the room. This is a tight family and each is willing to fight for the other.

I especially like Abby. She came right up to me after giving Walt a huge hug and stabs me in the chest with her index finger. "Listen to me, buddy. Gina's the closest thing I have to a sister so you better be on your game at all times, got me? If I think for one minute that you're slacking off then he" —she points to Walt— "gets what's left of you after I'm done fucking you up. Make no mistake, Cole. I *will* fuck you up."

I looks at her husband, Max. He smirks and shrugs.

"I get it, Abby. No worries."

She walks back to Gina, muttering about how I better be worried.

Next, Carina looks me up and down. She speaks to Walt. "This is your best? He seems a little small, no?"

Small? Next to her husband and brother in law, I am freaking *Gulliver*!

Walt chuckles. “He’s very well trained, Carina.”

She rolls her eyes and whispers something to Ray, who nods, never taking his eyes off me.

Yeah. This is going to be fun.

GINA

I need to get out. The realization that I caused Nick's death suffocates me. All around me, my family is talking about Cole and creating his backstory as my cousin. There is too much noise. I need to clear my head.

I quietly slip into my room and close the door. Kicking off my shoes, I crawl under the covers and curl into a ball on my side. Memories of Nick flood my head. I didn't realize I started crying until the tears are wiped from my eyes.

"Don't cry, sweetheart."

Opening my eyes, Cole smiles down at me. "It's a bit overwhelming, huh?" He rubs small circles across my back.

"It's my fault."

Cole's eyes harden and his hand stills. "No, it's not. You aren't responsible for someone else's actions."

I sit up and shake my head. "You don't understand." I draw my knees to my chest, wrapping my arms around them.

Cole closes his eyes and sighs. "Gina, you couldn't have known that someone was going to hurt Nick. No one saw it coming."

The tears are back. I sniffle. "But if I didn't—"

"No." Cole's tone brokers no argument. He grasps my chin and looks me in the eye. "It's. Not. Your. Fault."

COLE

All I want to do is scoop Gina up and take away her pain, but I know that can't happen.

This is a job. I'm not supposed to get emotionally involved, but damn it, there is something about her that makes my inner caveman growl.

I try to convince her that Nick's death isn't her fault, but I can tell she doesn't believe me.

Gina says she is tired. I rise to leave.

"Will you stay with me?"

I am shocked, but take my suit jacket off, toe off my shoes, and slide into the bed with her. Gina curls into my side and rests her head on my chest. "I'm so tired."

I run my hand up and down her back. "Rest. I've got you."

She sighs and relaxes. After a few minutes, her breathing evens out and she falls asleep.

A few minutes later, Abby comes into the room. She stops and takes in the scene. Giving me a nod and a smile, she backs out of the room and quietly closes the door.

I continue to run my hand up and down Gina's back. Her hair smells like almonds. I inhale deeply. She is tiny, but fits perfectly against me.

She shows incredible strength considering all that has happened to her. My gut churns at the thought of her being in so much pain. Anger at the thought of someone hurting her makes my body stiffen. Gina lets out a soft murmur and frowns in her sleep. I relax and once again stroke her back. She shifts again and settles with a sigh.

I am screwed.

GINA

Sunlight streams across my face. I groan. I forgot to pull the shades when I went to bed yesterday. When I try to move, an arm tightens around my waist. Memories of the night before rush back at me. I look over my shoulder at a sleeping Cole.

He looks even better than the day before. His hair is mussed and the stubble along his jawline seems darker.

I reach out and stroke his chin. His eyes snap open.

"Hey."

I shift out of his embrace, moving to the edge of the bed. "Hey. Thanks for staying with me last night."

He sits up and runs a hand over his head, making his hair spike up in places. "No problem. Did you sleep well?"

His question makes me pause. "Actually, it was the first night without any nightmares."

He appears pleased by my answer. “Good. I’m going to make some coffee and unpack.” He turns to leave, grabbing his suit jacket from the end of the bed.

“Wait, what do you mean unpack? You’re staying *here*?”

His eyebrows draw together. “Yeah. That’s part of my cover story. I’m your cousin and I’m staying here. I’m even going to be working downstairs.”

I jump out of bed and pace. “The hell you are! Who decided this?” I grab my phone off the nightstand and make a call.

“Dad? Why is Cole living with me and working downstairs?”

“Good morning, sweetie. Did you sleep well?”

I plant a fist on my hip and glare at Cole. He chuckles as he walks out the door.

“Quit stalling, Dad, and spill it.”

He sighs. "Walt and I thought it would be best for you to stay in your apartment as long as someone stayed with you."

"No."

His voice hardens. "It wasn't a question, Gina. It's been decided."

I pace my room again, anger building. "Oh, really? You do realize that I'm an adult and not some child you can boss around, right? I can make my own decisions and I say Cole goes."

"That's fine. If Cole goes, then I will be there in twenty minutes to pack you up and bring you home."

I stop pacing and wave my arm in the air. "You can't just make decisions for me anymore!"

I sigh. "Dad, I get it. Everyone wants me safe, but honestly I'm a big girl and can take care of myself."

"Gina, those are your choices. Which is it? Cole or home?"

Cole walks in with a steaming cup of coffee. He puts it on my nightstand, gives me a wink, and walks out.

I pick up the mug and take a sip. Damn, that is good.

"I guess Cole stays."

Dad blows out a breath. "Good. Walt assured me he's a good man and good at what he does. If he tries anything inappropriate with you, though . . . ."

I laugh. "I know, you'll kill him."

My dad chuckles. "Nah, I'll let Abby kill him."

I take another sip of coffee and sigh. "Thanks, Dad."

"*Ti amo, bambina*."

"*Anch'io ti amo*, Dad."

I hang up and wander into the living room. Cole sits on the couch. He had changed into a fresh pair of jeans and a black t-shirt that molds to every muscle on his broad chest. His shoes are off and his hair is damp.

He sips from a steaming mug. "So do I need to repack my stuff?"

I sit on the opposite end of the couch and tuck my feet under me. “No. Looks like we’re going to be roommates for a while.”

He studies me for a moment. “How do you feel about that?”

I shrug. “You make a decent cup of coffee, so that’s good.”

“Decent, huh?” A smile tugs his lips.

I hold out my hand and wiggle it from side to side. “Meh.”

Cole chuckles.

“We’re going to need some ground rules.”

Cole nods and shifts to face me. “Agreed.”

I put my mug on the coffee table and count off on my fingers. “First of all, I won’t clean up after you. You make a mess, you clean it. That includes your room and your bathroom”

“Okay.”

“Next, I’m not your wife. I won’t be doing your laundry or cooking for you.”

He shrugs. “I can cook.”

My eyes widen. “Really? You any good? Because I suck at it. When Abby lived here, she did all the cooking.”

Cole smiles. “I’ll make you a deal, I’ll cook and you clean the dishes.”

“I’ll need to taste your skills before I agree to that.”

Cole chuckles. “Fair enough. We’ll go shopping today for groceries and I’ll cook for you tonight.”

“Finally, I don’t want you bringing women back here for any . . . activities. This is my home and I don’t do small talk with skanks and whores.”

Cole’s eyebrows shoot up. “Skanks and whores? Is that who you think I date?”

I shrug and pickup my mug. “I don’t know who or what you date and I don’t care. I just don’t want it in my house.”

He stands and puts his hands in his front pockets. "Fair enough. Now I have some rules of my own."

I sip my coffee and raise an eyebrow. "Do you now?"

"Yes and they *will* be followed," he challenges.

I put my mug down and smile sweetly, my voice full of sarcasm. "Oh, do tell."

Ignoring me, Cole lays out his rules.

"First, you and I will have to act like family, which means we're going to be spending a lot of time together. We need to at least pretend to get along."

I shrug. He continues.

"Second, I am to know where you are at all times. I prefer you not go out of the apartment or restaurant without me."

I snort and mutter under my breath.

"Lastly, I want to chip you."

"Excuse me?"

He goes to his room and returns with a small vial. He hands it over. I peer inside. There is a small piece of metal in it.

"What the hell is this?"

He sits next to me on the couch. "It's a small microchip that is implanted right under the skin. It doesn't hurt. It's so Walt's tech guys and I can track your movements when I'm not with you."

I spring to my feet, throwing the vial at Cole's head. "Are you freaking kidding me? You want to chip me like a *dog*?"

Cole sighs. "I told Walt you'd have a problem with this."

"You're damn right I have a problem with this." I fling my arms in the air. "I have a problem with all of this, and that" —I point to the vial— "is *never* going to happen!"

I stomp to my room and slam the door.

"Son of a bitch!" I pick up a shoe and throw it across the room.

I throw on some clothes and shove my feet into a pair of low heels. I'd had enough.

"Where are you going?" Cole watches me gather my purse.

My hand grips the front doorknob as I jerk the door open. "Out."

I slam the door behind me and head downstairs. I get into my car and scream as I slap the steering wheel. The passenger side door opens and Cole slides into the seat.

"What did the steering wheel ever do to you?" He flashes a grin.

"Get out of my car," I seethe.

"No can do, *cousin*."

I glare at him. He smiles. It is infuriating. "Dannato figlio di puttana di madre."

Cole laughs. "Did you just call me the son of a motherless whore?"

I gasp. "You understood that?"

“Sì, sono fluente in italiano, spagnolo, e francese.”

“Shit,” I mutter.

“So where are we going?” His seatbelt clicks into place.

I sigh and sink into my seat. “I hadn’t really thought that part out. I tend to get emotional and just react.”

Cole snickers. “You don’t say.”

I glare at him, but my temper is receding. “Shut up. Guess we’re going shopping, Chef Boy-Ardee.”

We drive to the local grocery store in relative silence. Cole takes the lead in the store, selecting produce, meats, and other essentials.

“How do you know I don’t have those already?” He loads several spices into the cart.

“I checked out your kitchen this morning when I made coffee. I was surprised to only find basic spices in there.”

I reach for a box of granola. “Like I said, Abby did the cooking when we lived together. She must have taken all that stuff with her when she left.”

Cole grabs a box of oatmeal and tosses it in the cart. “What can you cook?”

I push the cart down the aisle and reach for a loaf of wheat bread. “Toast.”

Cole puts my wheat bread back and grabs a loaf of multi-grain. I roll my eyes and put the wheat bread back in the cart.

“That’s all you can make?”

I stop to inspect the yogurt and toss a few into the cart. “I can make the basics, but I don’t like to cook. I would rather go shopping or read a book. Besides, if I get desperate I can always eat downstairs. Abby and Uncle Ray keep the fridge stocked.” I shrug.

“Your mom never taught you?”

We head toward the checkout line. “She tried, but it wasn’t something I ever wanted to learn. When Abby showed an interest in cooking, my mom focused on teaching her.”

I pull out my wallet, but Cole waves me off. “I’ve got it.”

I frown. “At least let me pay for my stuff.”

“No.”

I try to give the cashier money, but Cole glares and she refuses to take it.

“I’ll pay next time.”

He takes his change and stuffs it in his jeans. “We’ll see.”

We almost make it out of the store when a voice calls, “Gina, is that you?”

I stiffen. Walking toward us is Tina Brooks. Tina and I went to high school together. She is the quintessential cheerleader type—blonde hair, blue eyes, perfect figure. I hate her. She eyes Cole, her perfect white smile blinding.

“I thought that was you. How are you?” She glanced at me, extending her hand to Cole. “Tina Brooks.”

Cole takes her hand and kisses her knuckles. “Cole Ferretti.”

“My, what a charming man you have, Gina.”

Cole chuckles. “Oh no, Tina. Gina and I aren’t dating. I’m her cousin.”

I cringe, and then quickly smile. “Yes, Cole’s a cousin from my mom’s side. He heard about Nick and came to spend some time with me.”

Tina’s face morphs from a smile to a frown. She grabs my hands. I want to pull back, but don't. “Poor you, losing Nick to a freak accident like that. Such a shame. How are you?”

Her sincerity is a complete sham, but I nod, yanking my hands back. “It’s been hard, but everyone’s been so great. Now that Cole’s here, I think the healing will begin.”

Cole stiffens at my side, but the lazy smile never leaves his face.

Tina nods and plasters on a smile. “Well, if you need me, you know where to find me.” She turns and smiles brightly. “Cole, I hope to see you around, too.”

He nods. Tina heads toward her car. The exaggerated sway of Tina’s hips as she walks away makes me shudder. Cole pops the trunk and we load in the grocery bags. He runs the cart back while I start the car.

He slides into the passenger seat with a grin. “So you and Tina, BFFs?”

I playfully smack him on the arm. “Ah, no.”

“So I guess asking her out would be a bad idea then?”

I glance over to see if he is serious. “Remember what I said earlier about skanks and whores?”

“Yes.”

I shrug. “Consider yourself warned.”

Cole throws his head back and laughs. “Point taken.”

We drive home in comfortable silence. After pulling into my regular spot in the parking lot, I pop the trunk and grab for a bag, but Cole stops me.

“I’ll get them, but I want to check things out first.” He closes the trunk and takes my keys.

“Stay behind me, okay?”

I nod and follow. Cole checks the back door before inserting the new key and opening it. At the top of the stairs, he does the same thing. “Stay here.” He checks all the rooms before I get the "all clear" and am allowed in.

“I’ll be right back with the bags.”

He jogs down the stairs while I wander into the kitchen. I open up the wine chiller and take out an open bottle of Pinot. Pouring myself a healthy glass, I take a sip as Cole comes into the kitchen.

Holy hell.

He had loaded all of the bags between his two arms to carry them all at once. The muscles bulge under his t-shirt. I sputter into my wine. Cole drops the bags and pounds on my back. “Are you alright?”

I cough and wave him away. “Fine,” I croak. “Just went down the wrong pipe.”

He smirks and begins to put away the groceries. I am impressed that he knows where everything goes.

“Just how much snooping did you do this morning?”

He flashes me that lazy smile I’d come to like. “Enough.”

Cole unpacks the produce; there are all the fixings for an amazing salad, but what surprises me is when he pulls out a jar of capers.

“What’s for dinner?”

“Chicken Piccata and salad.”

“Wow. I’m impressed.”

Cole roots through the drawers until he finds the meat mallet. “Don’t be too impressed. You’re going to help.”

I laugh. “Yeah, right.”

He hands me an apron. Next he grabs a large cutting board and places it on the counter in front of me. "Yeah, you are."

I narrow my eyes. "That wasn't the deal."

Cole chuckles. "So sue me." He grabs the apron and stands behind me. "Allow me." He whispers in my ear, causing shivers to run down my spine.

His hands linger just a moment on my hips after he ties the bow at my waist. He puts his nose in my hair and inhales deeply. When I turn to face him, there is no mistaking the desire in his eyes.

"So, um, what is it you want me to do?"

His nostrils flare. Part of me hopes he will say something completely outrageous and inappropriate.

Cole keeps his features passive as he stares at me. He gives my hips a gentle squeeze and turns away. "I'm assuming you can put together a salad for us?"

I tilt my head. "Why would you assume that?"

He slowly looks me up and down. I squirm under his heated gaze. “Because you’re in great shape and I assume eating healthy is part of your routine. Besides, Abby told me making salads was something you excelled at downstairs.” He winks before handing me a head of lettuce.

I smirk and grab a knife. “Do you really think busting my chops while I’m holding a weapon is the right move here?”

Again his gaze rakes over my body. “I’ll take my chances.”

My face flushes. I grab the lettuce from his outstretched hand. I move to the far end of the kitchen to put some distance between my hormones and the sexy man in my kitchen.

I shake my head. What am I doing? Nick is barely cold in the ground and I am fantasizing about Cole. Surely I am going to hell.

“Where’d you go just now?”

I glance up. Cole looks concerned. “Are you alright?”

“Fine. Just lost in my own world for a moment. It’s nothing.”

Cole unwraps the chicken. “Didn’t look like nothing. You looked sad. I don’t like that look on your face.”

I am surprised. “I was just thinking about Nick, sorry.”

Cole grabs another cutting board, laying the chicken on top of it. He trims the pieces with expert knife skills. “How long were you two together?” His eyes never leave the board.

I resume chopping the lettuce. “About three years.”

Cole looks up, his knife resting at the edge of the board. “That’s a long time to be with someone. You must have really loved him. It’s understandable that you’re sad.”

I can't meet his eyes. “I guess.”

“You guess?”

I transfer the lettuce to the bowl and grab the carrots. “I mean we were together a long time and I did love him, but I'm not sure if I was still in love with him. Does that make sense?"

Cole sighs. "I get that. Sometimes you stay together because it's more habit than anything else."

"Sounds like you have some experience in this area."

He pounds the chicken into thin pieces and arranges it in the pan. "Not me, my sister. She calls it the *shoe theory*."

Putting my own knife down, I reach for my wine glass. "What's that?"

A smile tugs his lips. "Well, according to my sister, the shoe theory states that once you've *broken in* someone, they become like a pair of well-worn shoes. The shoes may get old and ratty, but you don't want to get rid of them because they're familiar, comfortable, and the thought of breaking in a new pair is too hard."

I sip my wine, contemplating what Cole said. It is difficult to admit that he is right in his assessment of mine and Nick's relationship; it was familiar and comfortable. We fell into a routine and the spark dimmed. Right before he died, we had a small spark, but even then I tried to decide if I wanted to continue our relationship.

I pick up the knife and cut the rest of the vegetables in silence.

COLE

Damn it.

I fucked that up royally. One minute we are having a good time and being silly, the next Gina withdraws into herself.

Biting back a curse, I watch Gina finish the salad, grab her refilled wine glass, and walk out of the kitchen without a word.

When dinner is ready I plate the meal and walk into the living room. Gina is sitting on the couch, her legs tucked under her, sipping her wine. There are a few glowing candles giving the room a serene, romantic feel. I didn't realized I was staring until she smiles.

“That smells amazing.”

I put the plates on the table and cross to her in three long strides. Her eyes widen as I take her wine glass from her and place it on the coaster on the coffee table. She smiles slightly, watching my movements. I make a mental note to always use a coaster. Reaching down, I grasp her hands in mine and gently lift her from the couch. Her breathing hitches when our hands connect.

"I've wanted to do this since the first moment I saw you."

I lean down and gently brush my lips over hers. Gina stiffens for a second. I am afraid I messed up again, but she softens under my grasp and leans in. I groan when her hips push into mine. I feel her nipples pebble against my shirt.

I groan and deepen the kiss. As my tongue sweeps her bottom lip, she opens for me. She tastes like the wine in her glass; crisp with a touch of sweet. My hands travel to her hair. I double-fist her long, thick locks and give a slight tug. Gina's breath catches a second before she moans again.

So she likes it a little rough; good to know.

I tear my mouth from her, trailing kisses down her neck. My hands roam from her hair down her back. I grasp her firm, round ass. She grinds into my erection. I hiss.

"Baby, I think we better stop."

I take a step back; there is no mistaking the hurt in her eyes. "Oh. Right" She looks down, her hair forming a curtain around her face.

Shit.

"Gina, don't do that. Don't hide from me."

She glances up, but quickly looks back at her toes. The lust in her eyes only a moment ago is gone.

"Baby, I want nothing more than take you into your bedroom right now and sink so deep into you that you forget everyone else but me, but I can't."

She nods. "I get it. It's a job. *I'm* a job. That means hands off." She reaches for her wine glass before heading toward her bedroom.

"Wait, at least eat something."

She turns and gives me a sad smile. “Thanks, but I’m not hungry. I’m sorry you went to all the trouble. Leave the dishes, I’ll do them tomorrow. Please feel free to help yourself to anything in the kitchen, but you don’t need to cook for me anymore. It’s not a job requirement.” She turns and retreats to her room. When the lock clicks into place, I know she isn't coming back out.

Double shit.

GINA

God, I'm so stupid.

I practically throw myself at Cole and he has to be the one to stop it. I never should have let him kiss me in the first place, but damn can that man *kiss.* I touch my still swollen lips as tears fall from my eyes. Nick is barely cold in the ground. There is also the matter of some crazed stalker trying to claim me and what am I doing? Trying to make out with the guy who is supposed to be protecting me! God, what is next? Sleep with Marco? I shake my head. It is only seven-thirty, but the thought of going back out and facing Cole is too painful. I take a quick shower and settle into bed.

I awake a few hours later as a scream tears from my throat. I sit straight up in bed, clawing at the air. Someone tries to break down my bedroom door. I roll out of bed, grabbing my Smith & Wesson from the nightstand. Earlier today I put it there in case the stalker comes back. The door splinters open. I fire. My attacker drops to the ground, but I don't know if he is hit or not.

“Gina? Shit! You fucking *shot* me!”

Wait, I know that voice.

“Cole?”

He gives a pain-filled laugh. “Yeah, baby. Put the gun down, okay? Shit, that hurts.”

I drop my gun on the bed and run to him. Cole is lying on the floor, holding onto his left side. Blood soaks his shirt and forms a small pool on the carpet.

“Oh my God, Cole!” I run into the bathroom and grab a towel. I run back, turning on the bedroom light. Cole is sickly pale. The pool of blood under him grows by the second. I hold the towel over the wound and apply pressure. Cole groans. I grab my cell phone. I call 911 first, then my dad.

“I guess you really are a good shot, huh?” Cole wheezes.

"Shit." I roll him slightly, he cries out in pain. "Cole I need to see the wound." There is an exit hole in his back. Thank God for small miracles. "It was a through and through, Cole, It should be okay."

Cole closes his eyes. His breathing is labored. The ambulance tears into the back lot. I run to the window. My dad is right behind them. He brings them to the bedroom and stops when he sees Cole.

Dad grabs me and checks me over. "Are you alright? Are you shot, too?"

I shake my head as the paramedics assess Cole. "The blood's not mine, Daddy."

"Did someone try and hurt you? Who shot Cole?"

I hear the paramedics say something about a collapsed lung. I start to cry. "I did. I shot him. It was an accident! I was having a nightmare and Cole was trying to get to me. I locked my door and when he broke it down, I shot him. I was still scared from the dream and forgot he was the good guy."

“We have to go, now!” The paramedics load Cole onto a stretcher. His eyes are closed and there is an oxygen mask on his face. His shirt is ripped off and one of the paramedics applies pressure to Cole’s side. His skin is sickly pale.

I tear from my father’s embrace and follow the stretcher to the ambulance. One of the paramedics stops me as I try to climb into the ambulance.

“I’m sorry, miss, but the police are on their way and they need to question you. You can’t go with us.”

They load Cole into the ambulance, close the doors in my face, and speed out of the lot. Seconds later, a police cruiser pulls into the lot. A uniformed man, along with a detective, exit the vehicle. I recognize the detective. He is a regular customer at the restaurant.

“Detective Michaels, I shot my cousin, Cole Ferretti, by accident.”

The look of surprise on the patrolman’s face is almost comical. Detective Michaels pulls out a small notebook and sighs. “Alright, Gina. Start at the beginning.”

Detective Michaels questions me and checks all my gun permits as well as my license to carry a concealed weapon. He assures me that as long as Cole corroborates my story, no charges will be filed. He did make me put my gun back into the closet safe, which is probably a good idea.

An hour later, my father and I run through the emergency doors. The whole family is already there, but there is no news.

My dad and Carina pass out coffee while I pace the waiting room for what feels like the millionth time. Everyone else sits on uncomfortable orange and yellow plastic chairs waiting for news.

Everyone is quiet. The scene is too familiar; the whole family in a hospital waiting room. We did it too many times in the last year.

Uncle Ray comes over and pulls me into a hug. "Bella, he'll be fine. He's a good man and we have all been praying for him."

I nod, not trusting my voice.

"I'm sorry, Bella."

I gaze into the warm chocolate eyes so much like my own. "Why?"

Uncle Ray kisses the crown of my head, murmuring into my hair, "You have been through too much for someone so young. You and Mio Angelo deserve happiness, not pain. First it was me, then Nick, and now Cole. It's too much."

I hug my uncle. "It's not your fault, Uncle Ray. It's mine. At least, Nick and Cole are my fault."

An arm snakes around my shoulders. Abby gives me a slight squeeze. "Oh, honey. You need to stop that. You aren't responsible for Nick's death and Cole getting shot was an *accident*."

I step back. "It's still my fault."

Abby grabs my hands. "Then I guess my parent's deaths are my fault."

I gasp. "How can you say that?"

She shrugs. “I should have tried harder to stop my father from leaving the house that day. If I had, he wouldn’t have driven drunk and gotten into the accident that caused their deaths.”

I grasp Abby’s shoulders and squeeze. “Abby, you were a kid. You couldn’t possibly know what was going to happen. It was a freak accident that your father’s car collided with your mom’s as she was coming home from work. It wasn’t your fault”

Abby smiles. “If that’s the logic we’re working with, you need to recognize the fact that Nick’s death wasn’t your fault, either. You didn’t rig the air nailer any more than I put the car keys in my father’s hand.”

I sigh. “And Cole?”

“Sweetie, you were defending yourself against what you thought was an attacker. Even the police aren’t going to press charges against you.”

I open my mouth to protest when the waiting room doors open and a tired doctor heads toward us.

"Mr. and Mrs. Toriello?"

Mom shoots to her feet. "How's Cole?"

The doctor smiles and my knees give out. Max grabs me before I hit the floor.

"He's going to be just fine. The bullet grazed the bottom of his lung, but didn't do any permanent damage. He was very lucky. A few inches higher and we would be having a very different conversation."

My dad shakes the doctor's hand. "Thanks, doctor. When can we see him?"

The doctor checks his watch. "He's sedated. He will be asleep for the next few hours. My advice is to go home and get some rest. Come back in the morning."

Mom gives the doctor a hug. "Thank you for what you did for my nephew."

For a brief moment I feel like Cole really is family.

The doctor reddens and smiles. "My pleasure, Mrs. Toriello. Have a good night."

He turns and walks back through the doors.

Max gives me a slight squeeze. “Feel better?”

I stand tall and smile for the first time since this nightmare began. “Not yet. Not until I see him with my own eyes.”

I settle into an orange chair. Dad sits next to me. “I think you should come home with your mom and me tonight. We can come back and see Cole in the morning.”

“No.”

He sighs. “I was afraid you were going to say that.” He settles into the chair.

“Dad, go home and get some sleep. I’ll be fine.”

He closes his eyes, leans his head on the wall behind us, and crosses his arms over his chest. “I’m fine right here with you.”

I give Mom a pleading look, but it is Uncle Ray who comes to my rescue. “Vince, go home and get some rest.

I'll stay with Bella and wait. We'll call you if anything changes."

Dad doesn't even open his eyes. "She's my daughter, Ray."

Uncle Ray plants his feet and squares his shoulders. "I know that, asino, but she is my niece and I owe her. Go home."

I am confused. "Uncle Ray, you don't owe me anything."

He smiles and cups my chin with his hand. "Si, Bella, I do. Not too long ago, you were all in this waiting room because I was selfish and didn't take care of myself the way I should have. Now it's my turn to repay and wait with you."

My dad sighs, opening one eye. "Ray, it's not necessary."

Ray's eyes harden as he glares at my father. "You're going to deny me this? Not allow me to repay a debt?"

My mom grabs my dad's hand and gently pulls him up. "No, Ray. We are grateful and accept your help. Consider the debt wiped clean."

Uncle Ray nods at his sister before he swings his eyes to my father. "Vince?"

My father nods and the men embrace. Abby smiles with tears in her eyes while Max holds her to his side.

Everyone kisses us goodnight and leaves. Ray hands Carina a key and whispers something into her ear. She smiles and nods before leaving with the rest of the family.

Uncle Ray and I sit back down and wait.

COLE

Pain.

All I feel is pain in my chest. I try to breath, but the pain is too intense. I crack open one eye and check out the room. I am in a hospital. Memories of Gina shooting me came rushing back. I try to sit up, but sink back on the pillows from the pain.

“Oh, honey. You shouldn’t be moving around like that. Hang on.”

The middle aged nurse smiles down at me. Her hair is bright red and hangs down her back in a long braid. She wears *Scooby-Doo* scrubs. I try to chuckle, but end up groaning.

“My name is Lauren. I’ll be your day nurse. Sorry about the scrubs. I usually work on the children’s ward. Let me adjust your bed.”

Lauren adjusts my bed so I am sitting up a little more. She hands me a cup of water and I am grateful. The cold water feels good passing over my dry lips. I have tubes up my nose. I pull to take them out and get my hands slapped.

“Those need to stay in, hon, at least until the doctor sees you. The police have been here all morning waiting to talk to you. Can I send them in?”

I nod and she leaves. Two detectives come in and ask questions about the “incident.” Apparently my story matches what Gina told the police. I am relieved to hear that Gina isn't facing any charges. After the police leave, my doctor and Lauren come back in. The doctor tells me that I need to stay in the hospital for a few more days and the tubes need to stay in for at least one more day. I am surprised to hear the extent of my injuries and grateful Gina didn’t kill me.

When the doctor leaves, Lauren stays behind. She smiles and adjusts my pillows. “There’s been a girl and her uncle here all night waiting to see you. I told them this morning that we'd call with any changes, but she refused to leave. She said her name was Gina. Do you want to see her?"

My chest tightens. She stayed all night?

"Yes, please."

Lauren winks on her way out the door. Moments later, Gina flies into the room. She looks exhausted, purple circles rim her eyes. Gina takes one look at me and bursts into tears.

"Cole. Oh, God. I'm so sorry!"

I wave her over. She sits in the chair next to my bed. She puts her head down on the edge of the bed. The bed shakes slightly from her sobs. "I didn't know it was you, I swear!"

I run my hand over her head, trying to soothe her. "Shh. Gina, it's alright. I'm fine, really. I'm sorry I scared you."

She lifts her head, her eyes are red and puffy, but in that moment she looks beautiful to me.

“C’mere.” I shift to make room for her on the bed. Gina shakes her head, but I insist. “Baby, please. I need to feel you beside me.”

She carefully slides onto the bed so as to not disturb the wires attached to me and lays her head in the crook of my arm. I run my hand up and down her spine and soon she is asleep. Ray comes in a few moments later and takes in the scene. He nods once and walks out. Lauren comes in next. She frowns at Gina in my bed but there is a sparkle in her eye. She doesn't attempt to wake Gina to move out of bed. Instead she points between Gina and me and whispers, “No hank-panky young man.” I smirk and give her a small salute. Lauren turns off the light and closes the door. I continue to rub Gina’s back until I too fall asleep.

I awake some time later. Opening my eyes, I see that Gina is still asleep. Someone clears their throat and my eyes swing to the left. Vince sits in a chair near my bed. He does not look happy.

“So this is how you keep things professional?”

I sigh. “Vince, professional flew out the window the second Gina opened the door that first day.”

He stands and paces the room. Gina does that, too. I smile at their similarities.

“I think I should call Walt and have someone else sent here.”

I freeze. “No.”

Vince stops pacing and glares at me. “I wasn’t asking for your permission, Cole.”

I glare right back. “I won’t leave her, Vince.”

He waves his arms around. “Look at you! You can’t even stop yourself from getting shot, how can you protect my daughter?”

“I’m. Not. Leaving.”

Gina stirs under my arm and mumbles, “He stays, Daddy. Cole makes me feel safe.”

A triumphant smile spreads across my face as Vince sits back in his chair and swears in Italian.

Gina sits up and smiles at me. “How are you feeling?”

“Better.”

She kisses me on the cheek then carefully crawls out of bed. I miss her instantly.

“Where are you going?”

She glances at her father. “Dad and I are going to get coffee.”

Vince stops cursing and raises an eyebrow. “We are?”

Gina grabs her father’s arm, pulling him from the chair. “Yup, and you’re buying. Let’s go.”

Vince sighs, but I see a smile tug the corner of his mouth.

“By the way Dad, Cole is fluent in Italian so he understood everything you just said about him."

Vince’s head whips in my direction. “Is that true?”

I chuckle. “Sì. Mia madre era in realtà una bella donna che non sarebbe affezionato a voi insultando suo figlio.”

Yes. My mother was actually a lovely woman who would not be fond of you insulting her son.

Gina winks at me before pulling a stunned Vince from the room. “Be back soon.”

GINA

“Dad, we need to talk.”

We take our coffees to a nearby table and sit. My father takes a sip and waits for me to continue.

I sigh. “I need your advice.”

His eyebrows quirk. “Okay.”

“I’m developing feelings for Cole and I feel like it’s too soon.”

He takes another sip of his coffee. “Why do you think that?”

I shrug. “Dad, Nick just died. I mean, what will people think?”

“Why do you care what people think?”

My shoulders slump. “I want to do what’s right.”

“Right for whom?”

I shrug, toying with the lid on my cup. "I don't know. You, Mom, the family, Nick, Cole."

My father grabs my hand. "I didn't hear you in that line-up."

"I don't want to disgrace the family."

My father's grip tightens, forcing me to look him in the eye. "Never in your life have you disgraced the family, Gina. Never."

My eyes mist. "I feel guilty for the feelings I have for Cole. Like I'm disrespecting Nick."

Dad laces his fingers with mine, his calloused thumb stroking mine. "I understand, honey, but Nick is gone. You can't stop living or loving because of that."

I take a deep breath and let it out. "You know, I usually go to Mom or Abby for this kinda stuff, but you made me feel better. Thanks, Dad."

He smiles. "Io amo e vi protegga ragazza per sempre, bambino." *I will love and protect you forever, baby girl.*

A tear slides down my cheek. Dad wipes it away. "Now let's go see what's going on with Cole."

***

Cole stays in the hospital for three more days. The doctors want to be sure his lung function is normal and he doesn't develop an infection. I stay with him for those three days. Abby is kind enough to bring me some toiletries and clothes. I shower in Cole's bathroom. He curses every time I go in alone. I even sleep in Cole's hospital bed. He claims he sleeps better knowing I am with him and not home alone; truth be told, I sleep better those nights, too.

We spend our days talking and playing twenty questions.

"What's your favorite ice cream flavor?"

Cole thinks for a moment. "I guess Rocky Road although Mint Chip is pretty close to the top of the list."

"Favorite color?"

He caresses my cheek. “It was green but since I’ve met you I have an increased fondness for the same shade of brown as your eyes.”

I blush as my heart melts.

“Favorite kind of movie?”

“Action of course, I am a guy after all.”

I learn everything about Cole. His real name is Colton Taylor. He is twenty-eight and is from North Carolina, where his parents still live. He has an older sister, Jane, and a younger step- brother, Dennis. Cole’s mom died of cancer when he was fifteen. His dad got remarried right after Cole graduated from high school. Jackie is a nice woman whom Cole loves very much. Jackie’s son Dennis was six when she married Cole’s dad. He is sixteen now. Cole says they speak at least once a week. Cole’s older sister is married and living in Seattle with her husband, who is doing his residency in a hospital out there. They don't have any children yet since Jane is working on her PhD in psychology.

I also learned that Cole has a degree in criminal justice. Walter personally sought out Cole to join his organization. Cole is a weapons expert and knows how to fly small planes thanks to his military training as a former SEAL.

He is also a bit of a card shark. He beat the pants off of me in poker—actually he suggests we play strip poker, but since he is still in the hospital, I veto that idea. That is when I discovered that Cole is absolutely adorable when he pouts.

Our days are spent talking and laughing and our nights are spent kissing and exploring. It is difficult. There's never much privacy in the hospital, but we make it work. We don't have sex, but we have fun kissing and fondling. I am falling in love with Cole. It exhilarates and scares me. What if he gets hurt again because of me or dies like Nick? Those thoughts keep me awake long after Cole falls asleep at night.

When he is released from the hospital, I insist Cole comes home with me. Walter offers me another associate to take Cole's place until he is fully healed. I put my foot down and refuse another associate. Walter and my father don't like my decision, but they reluctantly agree.

By the time Cole's doctor sees him and all the paperwork is taken care of, it is almost dinner time. Cole is still a little sore, but he claims to be fine. We decide to go home rather than go out to eat. When we pull into the parking lot behind the restaurant, Cole's eyes light up. I had arranged with Walter to have Cole's car delivered. His Audi TT Roadster is parked in my usual spot. I park across the lot. Cole quickly scrambles out of my car. He walks over and lovingly caresses the car, murmuring to himself.

The car is beautiful—sleek, black, and best of all, a convertible.

He turn, a smile on his face. "Did you do this?"

I nod. "I thought a drive might be nice before it gets too cold to put the top down. Walter said he left the keys under the visor."

Cole opens the door and gracefully slides into the driver's seat. Seconds later, the car roars to life. The top retracts and Cole waves to me. "C'mon, beautiful. Let's go for a spin."

I hop into the passenger seat and let out a whoop as Cole tears out of the lot.

COLE

I can't believe Gina arranged to have my baby delivered here. Taking a long drive is just what I need. Having her by my side is a bonus.

Grasping her hand, I bring her fingers to my lips for a soft kiss. “Thank you, Gina.”

She gives me a shy smile and giggles. I am instantly hard. Damn, I need to turn this car around. A drive was a great idea ten minutes ago. Now all I want is to explore every inch of Gina properly and hear her scream my name. Not paying attention to where I am going, I make a wrong turn and we end up on a residential street. Slowing to the speed limit, I look around the neighborhood. The houses are modest, but well kept. Toys and minivans litter almost every driveway. Gina stiffens in her seat. I glance over. She stares at a house. No, she is staring at a man on the porch of the house. I recognize him; Tommy Reynolds. He definitely likes Gina; if looks could kill, I'd be six feet under.

Gina lets out a gasp when I swing into Tommy's driveway. "What are you doing," she hisses.

Tommy cautiously comes over to the car. He stands about three feet from Gina's door.

"Hey, Gina." He gives her a smile before turning to glare at me. "Who's your friend?"

I get out of the car and walk over with my hand out. "Hi. I'm Cole, Gina's cousin."

Tommy features relax. "Cousin?" He takes my hand and gives it a formidable squeeze. "Tommy Reynolds. I'm Gina's friend from high school."

"Oh, right! The one who works for Uncle Ray."

Tommy nods. "That's me." He focused on Gina. "I didn't know your cousin was coming."

I step closer to the car. "Yeah. Aunt Ava called my mom about the trouble Gina's been having, so I thought I'd come for a visit."

Gina shifts in her seat, but gives Tommy a bright, although fake, smile. "That's right. Cole's between jobs right now. He thought he'd take some time off and hang out with me. He's staying in Abby's old room for now."

Tommy eyes the car. "Between jobs? What did you do, if you don't mind my asking?"

"I was in finance. I told rich people how to spend their money."

Tommy points to the car. "Looks like you did well for yourself, too."

Shrugging, I give Tommy a conspiratorial wink. "The car? That was a gift from a very *grateful* client."

Tommy laughs and relaxes some more. "Wow. Good for you, man."

Gina huffs. "*Eww*, Cole. Gross!" I smile at how well she plays her part.

Tommy chuckles and takes a step toward the car. He stuffs his hands in his front pockets. “So, Gina, I haven’t seen you in a while. Where’ve ya been?”

Gina shifts in her seat, unsure what to say. “Oh, um . . . .”

I take a step closer to Tommy. “Yeah, that’s my fault again. I took Gina to Atlantic City for a few days to see my mom. I figured a change of scenery might do her some good, ya know?” Tommy nodded. “We just got back this afternoon. Gina was showing me around town. I haven’t been here since . . .” I look at Gina.

“Probably since Nonna died when we were little.”

Damn, I am impressed with her ability to lie on the spot.

I laugh and shake Tommy’s hand. “I guess it has been a while. It was nice to meet you, Tommy. Guess I’ll see you around.”

Tommy smiles and waves as we pull out of the driveway. After we round the corner, I pull over and take out my phone. Walt answers on the second ring. "Yeah?"

"Walt, its Cole. We have a problem."

***

An hour later, we are gathered in Gina's living room. Walt is still in London, but I have him on Skype.

"Okay, Cole. Now that we're all here, what's going on?" Walt looks like he is asleep on his feet. He scrubs his hand down his face and stifles a yawn.

"I met Tommy Reynolds today."

Walt snaps. "Get to the point, Cole. I have shit to do here."

I look at Gina. "I think he killed Nick."

Gina squeezes her eyes shut. Ava gasps.

Walt sits up straighter. "How do you know?"

I sit and stare at Walt. “Gina and I were driving around today and we ended up on Tommy’s block. He was out in the yard, so I pulled in the driveway to do a little recon.”

Walt shakes his head. “Smart. And?”

I look over at Gina, but her eyes are still closed. Silent tears leak down her face. “I saw two nail guns on the porch. They had been disassembled to different points. I also noticed that all the windows facing the street were blacked out.” I turn to Ava and Vince. “Doesn’t he live with his father?”

Vince nods. Ava speaks up. “I think his father went away to visit a sister or something.”

I nod. “Boss, we need Tommy’s military records.”

He snorts. “I’ll have them to you within the hour.”

GINA

I knew it was my fault. Nick is dead because of me. Everyone says it isn't my fault, but it is. It feels like the walls are closing in on me. I stand and head toward the bathroom, but decide to get out altogether.

Grabbing my keys, I slip my phone in the inside pocket of my jacket and quietly slide out the door without being noticed.

Or so I think.

I slip the key into my car door. A voice whispers in my ear, “Did you think I would let you get away from me that easily?”

Pain rips through me. I fall into the arms of my assailant. Tommy holds me in one arm; a Taser in his other hand. The smile on his face sends a shiver down my spine. His eyes are wild. A low, sinister laugh rumbles in his chest.

The Taser connects with my chest. I want to scream. My last thought is of Cole before the darkness overtakes me.

COLE

After finishing with Walt, I need to talk to Gina. After a quick check of the apartment, I pull Vince aside.

"She's gone."

His head snaps up. "What the hell do you mean she's gone? Where did she go?"

I grimace. "I don't know. She must have slipped out while we were talking to Walt."

Vince runs a hand over his head. "Shit. Did you check downstairs?"

"Not yet. I'll go now."

I turn. Vince grabs my arm. "Be discreet. No need to panic Ava or Ray just yet."

I nod and head out. Once downstairs, I check the pizzeria, the restaurant, and the kitchen. I even check the damn walk-in fridge, but it is empty. I walk out to the parking lot. Gina's keys are hanging from her car door.

Shit.

I scan the parking lot and walk between the cars, but come up empty.

Double shit.

Gina is gone. I have to face her family and Walt.

I go back into the apartment and catch Vince's eye. I give him a slight shake of the head. He closes his eyes and curses. Ava notices and asks about Gina.

The room goes still.

Vince holds his wife's hand as he tries to keep her calm. "She must have slipped out unnoticed. We'll get her back Ava, I swear."

Vince hangs his head for a few seconds before he snaps his head up. "Her phone, can you track it?"

I make the call to Walt's IT team.

The guys pull up her record, but her phone must be off because they can't get a signal.

Ava calls Ray; seconds later he and Carina come bursting through the door. Ray scans the room and zeroes in on me. He is on me in three strides. For a little guy he is deceptively strong. "You have failed and now Bella is missing." He accentuates each word by slamming my head against the wall.

I let him seethe for another minute before I grab his shirt collar. "Kill me later. Let's go find Gina."

Ray looks at Carina. Not a word is spoken, but she nods and sits next to Ava, who is crying and shaking in Vince's arms. Vince stands, carefully shifting Ava into Carina's arms. I can't take Vince with me.

"Stay here. Call Walt and tell him I may need him. Then monitor the computer and call me if the cell phone becomes active."

Vince looks at Ray; again no words are spoken, but Ray nods and heads toward the door. This family and their non-verbal conversations are freaking me the fuck out.

We head down the stairs and hop into my car.

"Where to first?" Ray sits, staring straight ahead.

"First we check Tommy's house."

A call to the tech crew reveals that Tommy's father went to Arizona the week before Nick was attacked. The crew sends me in the information. I call Mr. Reynolds.

I put the phone on speaker in case I need Ray's input.

"Hello?"

"Mr. Reynolds?"

"Yes. Who is this?"

"Sir, my name is Cole. I'm a friend of Gina Toriello's."

Mr. Reynolds sucks in a breath. "Does Tommy have her?"

The look of shock on Ray's face mirrors my own. "We think so, sir."

"Damn it. I was afraid this would happen."

"Sir, we are pulling up to your house right now. We need to understand what's going on."

Mr. Reynolds sighs. "Tommy was a good soldier, best in his unit. His unit was attacked during a routine patrol. Tommy was the only one to survive. He lost his fiancée during the attack—she was in his unit. He blames himself. Tommy suffers from severe PTSD and an anxiety disorder since the attack. He's supposed to take his medication every day. He was doing a really good job with it so I felt comfortable leaving him when my sister called and asked me to help her after she had her hip replaced."

Shit.

"Sir, what happens if he doesn't take his medication?"

"He becomes delusional. He fixates on something and won't let go of it. In the VA hospital he became violent searching for his fiancée before they got his medications straight. He hasn't answered my calls for almost a week."

Ray is pissed. Right now his niece is in the hands of a mentally ill man with military training and it is entirely my fault.

"Sir, we need to get into your house to see if Tommy has Gina in there."

"I understand. I keep a spare key to the back door under the mat. Try not to hurt Tommy. He's a good boy, he just needs help."

"We'll try our best to keep him and Gina safe, sir."

"Thank you. I'm gonna let my sister know I have to go home and will be out on the next flight."

Mr. Reynolds hangs up. I glance at Ray. "Ready?"

He is already out of the car and half way up the driveway.

We find the key and head inside. The smell hits me first. The kitchen is full of the empty food containers. The garbage hasn't been taken out in at least a week.

"Jesus," Ray whispers. "I got a bad feeling about this, Cole."

I do, too. I draw my gun.

We quietly creep through the house, but no one is there. When we get to Tommy's bedroom, Ray lets out a stream of curses in Italian.

The wall opposite the bed is covered with pictures of Gina.

"That son of a bitch has been stalking her since he got home."

I holster my weapon and pick up a framed photo of Gina and Nick. Tommy has blacked out Nick's face.

Ray looks at the picture and swears some more. "Damn it, Gina was right. Tommy did kill Nick. This is gonna devastate his father."

I look around for clues as to where Tommy has taken Gina. I come across Tommy's medications in the bathroom. The prescriptions were filled three weeks ago, but the bottles are almost full.

I hold up the bottles for Ray to see. “Looks like he stopped taking them the day after his father left town.”

Ray’s face hardens. “Any idea where he took her?”

I shake my head and pull out my phone. Mr. Reynolds answer on the second ring.

“Did you find him?”

“No, Mr. Reynolds. The house is empty. Can you think of any place he might have taken her?”

The line is quiet for a minute. “I have a hunting cabin.”

My heart sinks. A hunting cabin means seclusion and weapons. Considering Tommy’s state of mind, that can be a deadly combination for Gina.

“Where’s the cabin, Mr. Reynolds?”

“Montague, New Jersey.”

I hang up and make a call to Walt. He picks up on the first ring. “Did you find her?”

“Not yet. We are at the Reynold's house. Tommy’s not here and it looks like he’s been off his meds for a while.”

“Shit. How bad is it?”

I don't sugar coat it for him. “Really fucking bad, Walt. His father mentioned a hunting cabin in Montague, New Jersey.”

Key strokes click in the background. “Got it. It’s a ninety-minute drive, but I can have wheels up in ten. Get to the landing strip.”

The Alexandria Airport is a few miles outside town. Ray and I are there in ten minutes to find a very frustrated Vince screaming into his phone and pacing the runway.

“What’s going on?”

“The fucking pilot is missing!”

“What do you mean he’s missing?”

Vince throws his phone into his pocket. “Walt is trying to find someone to get here and fly us. The pilot went on some kind of bender or something and his wife can’t find him.”

"Shit!" My phone rings. I answer and immediately hold it away from my ear, Walt is screaming. "He's so fucking fired! It looks like you're gonna have to fly today. It's only a twenty minute flight and then twenty-three minutes from the airport to the cabin. It's gonna be fucking close. I put the state police on alert up there, but it's a small barracks and they could only spare two officers. They'll be waiting for you when you land."

"Got it. I'll call you when we have her."

"Cole, I mean it when I say if anything happens to Gina, I won't have to hurt you. Ray and Vince will kill you."

"I know, Walt. Anything on her cell phone?"

Walt sighs. "Still off." He hangs up.

Ray is trying to calm Vince down. This is about to get ugly. Fucking pilot. If he shows up then it's just me going to New Jersey. Now I have to take one of them with me.

I run over to the plane—a small two-seater Cessna. I give a quick inspection. It is ready to go.

I jog over to where Ray and Vince are arguing.

"Here's the situation, I'm flying one of you up there with me. You have about three minutes to decide while I radio the tower with our flight plan."

Ray nods, but Vince's brows draw together. "What do you mean you're gonna fly this thing? Can you do that?"

I nod. "Yes, I'm military trained to fly for combat missions. I was a SEAL, sir."

Vince mutters, "Damn." I climb into to the cockpit to radio the tower. A minute later, Ray joins me.

I am shocked, but relieved it is him and not Vince. Ray seems more controlled in this type of situation. Vince's emotions could get him or Gina killed.

"Vince was afraid he would fuck something up," Ray says as if reading my thoughts. "Besides, you might have been a SEAL, but I'm really good with the wet work." He pulls two scary knives from his waistband. I am thankful he is on my side.

I start the plane and speed down the runway, hoping we won't be too late.

GINA

I open my eyes. Somewhere, I hear Tommy talking. I think someone else is in the car until I sit up. I am in the backseat of a car. My legs are bound at the ankles with duct tape and my wrists are bound behind my back. There is a piece of tape over my mouth and chin. My chest hurts from the Taser. There are burn marks on my shirt.

Tommy mutters to himself. “Ambushed. We shouldn’t have gone out. Told you to stay behind. Stubborn . . . bright bombs . . . screaming…” He slams his fist into the dashboard. “You had to go, didn’t you? Why didn’t you listen to me, Melissa? Huh? Why? You didn’t have anything to prove! I was supposed to keep you safe.” Tommy smiles at me in the rearview mirror. My blood runs cold.

“But now that you’ve come back to me, I can protect you. We can be a family just like you wanted, Melissa.”

I shudder. The sweet boy from high school is gone. I am trapped alone in a car in the dark with a madman. Trees race past as Tommy speeds down a country road. I'm not familiar with the surroundings. My arms feel like they are on fire as blood rushes into them. The feeling of pins and needles tells me that I've been lying on my side for a while. The dashboard navigation system says north. North? Where the hell is Tommy taking me? And who the hell is Melissa? I try to reach for the door handle, but can't grasp it with my hands bound together. I look around. There is nothing I can use as a weapon. All I can do is sit and wait. I pray that Cole will find me before Tommy kills me.

COLE

The flight is short. Ray and I are met at the airport by the two state troopers Walt told us about. They look fresh out of the academy. Ray gives me a pained look.

The taller of the two speaks first. "Gentlemen. My name is Joe Stanton and this is my partner, Mike Cruz. We have been advised to escort you to the cabin and await further instructions."

I glance over the officers. "Look, boys, as much as I appreciate your sense of protocol, waiting is not an option. My woman's life is at stake and we" —I motion between Ray and I— "will not be waiting for jack shit. So please take us to the cabin and then get the hell out of our way."

The troopers exchange a glance then they grin. Cruz speaks up. "We aren't too keen on following orders to the letter either, sir, which is why we got assigned to you. We're not here to get in your way and we want to help."

I blow out a breath and nod. "Good, let's go."

Ray and I pile into the backseat of the squad car as Joe fills us in on the situation.

"The cabin is pretty secluded. It's on a twelve acre lot that's set way back from the road. The cabin is in the middle of the lot and surrounded by woods."

Shit.

"Is there a way to get in unnoticed?" Ray looks out the car window at our surroundings.

Cruz nods. "There's a fire lane that runs along the back part of the property. That's our best bet. We can get pretty close, but we'll have to go on foot for part of it."

I nod. It is going to be tricky.

Joe says, "We looked at the cabin before we went to the airport. It was locked up tight, but we got a look inside. Three rooms. Only one door in and out. A few guns on the walls. We tried to pick the lock, but it's a double key deadbolt. We had no luck."

"I'm surprised you tried to break in, you had no warrant."

Cruz shrugs as he accelerates. "Like I said, we don't always follow the rules."

Ray grins. "I think I'm gonna like these boys."

GINA

We turn off the main road and bump our way down a dirt road. I am tossed from the ruts and cry out when my shoulder careens into the door handle.

"Only a little further, Melissa, and then we'll be safe."

I scream, but with the tape it came out a muffled cry.

"It's alright, sweetheart. They can't get us here. I'll protect you better this time, I promise."

My flesh breaks out in goose bumps.

We finally stop in front of an old cabin. Tommy gets out of the car and goes to the trunk. I try again to reach the door handle, but with my arms bound behind me, it is no use.

The backdoor swings open. Tommy yanks me from the car and cuts my leg restraints. He has on military fatigues and had a backpack slung over his shoulder.

"Let's get you settled and then I'll get the rest of the gear."

I stumble as the blood flow returns to my ankles. Tommy drops the backpack and supports my weight as we walk up the two steps to the door.

Tommy unlocks the cabin door. The room smells musty. Dust motes dance through the air when he turns on the lights.

The cabin is small. There is a main room with a couch, chair, and a small wood burning stove. To the left is a small kitchenette and two closed doors to the right. The room is illuminated by a single lamp next to the battered couch.

"The bathroom and the bedroom are over there." Tommy points to the two closed doors. "But why don't we sit in here for a while?" He leads me over to the chair and pulls out a switchblade. I shriek and shrink back, my eyes wide.

"*Shhh* . . . . It's alright, sweetheart. I'm not going to hurt you."

Tommy slices through the tape at my wrists. I rub them to get the circulation flowing again. He pulls out a set of zip-ties from his pocket. Tommy points to the only chair in the room. His eyes are unfocused and he starts to mumble something I can't understand. His hand holding the switchblade shakes. Sitting in the chair is my best option. . Tommy pulls out a set of zip ties and binds my wrists to the wooden arms of the chair. He leaves enough space so I won't lose blood flow to my wrists. I try to slip my hands through my restraints, but Tommy didn't leave enough slack for that. I struggle against my restraints and let out a frustrated grunt.

Tommy laughs. "I know you're mad at me, Melissa but it'll be fine. You'll see. The insurgents won't find us here."

I am more afraid Cole won't be able to find me, either.

Tommy goes back out to the car and comes in a few minutes later with the discarded backpack and a large plastic tub. He unpacks canned goods, K-rations, bottled water, batteries, and weapons. Lots of weapons. I count seven guns and four large knives. Tommy also wears a sidearm and has a large bowie knife tucked into his belt. There is only one window in the room we are in. I can't see out of it—the chair is purposefully moved out of the sightline.

Tommy opens a bottle of water as he walks toward me. “Melissa, are you thirsty?”

I nod. “I’m going to take the tape off as long as you’re not going to scream. If you do, the tape goes back on. Understand?”

I nod again. Tommy takes the tape off as gently as he can. I gasp for air when the tape is off my face. Tommy puts the bottle to my lips. I take a long swallow and he pulls the bottle back.

“That’s a good girl.”

“Tommy? Where are we?”

He runs a finger down my cheek. I suppress a shudder. “We’re safe, baby, and that’s all you need to know.”

“Tommy, who is after us?”

He looks confused for a moment. “The insurgents, of course. What’s wrong with you, Melissa?”

“Tommy, focus. Look at me. I’m Gina. Gina Toriello. I’m not Melissa. Do you hear me?”

Tommy thrusts his hands into his hair and violently shakes his head from side to side. “Stop lying, Melissa! The doctors told me you were dead. That you died with the rest of our unit that night, but they were wrong! You’re back and I’m going to keep you safe.”

At this moment I realize just how broken and disturbed Tommy is. I need him to calm down. The only way I will survive this is to play along and pray Cole finds us before Tommy kills me.

“I’m sorry, Tommy. I’m just afraid they’re going to get me again.”

Tommy lets go of his hair and drops to his knees in front of me, cupping my face in his hands. “I won’t let that happen again, baby. I’ll kill us both before I let that happen.”

“Tommy, baby, I can’t talk to you while you're pacing and waving that gun around. You’re scaring me. Can you put it down and untie me?”

Tommy thrusts his hands into his hair, covering his ears. “No! I can’t let you die again, Melissa. I can’t!”

I'm losing him. If I don't get free soon, I am as good as dead.

“Okay, Tommy. Keep the gun, but can you please untie me? I need to use the bathroom. Baby, you don’t want me to soil my clothes do you?”

A look of horror crosses his face. “Oh, Melissa. I’m so sorry. Of course you can go to the bathroom. I’ll cut you lose as long as you don’t try to leave, alright?”

I nod and give him a fake smile. “Tommy, I want to be with you. Why would I run?”

He sighs and takes out the switchblade. He cuts my arm restraints and the tape at my ankles.

I touch his cheek, trying to keep him calm. “Thank you, Tommy.”

He gathers me into his arms. “I love you, Melissa.”

COLE

We pull off the main road and access the fire lane. A few minutes later, Cruz turns off the car. “Okay, Cole. How do you wanna do this?”

Joe gets out of the car. Cruz pops the trunk. Ray and I walk to the back of the squad car. Ray lets out a low whistle. “Yup, I really like these guys.”

Joe and Cruz aren't fooling around. In the trunk are bullet proof vests, night vision goggles, and scoped assault rifles.

“Shit, Joe. You boys weren’t kidding about not following the rules.”

He grins as he hands Ray and I vests. “Strap on, boys, and let's go save your woman.”

Cruz puts on his flak jacket and pulls out a canister. “Flash bang. We’ll have about three minutes to get in and assess the situation once it goes off. The cabin's not that big, so it shouldn't take long."

Joe hands us small respirators. "When we get there, put these on. It'll protect you from the smoke."

Ray grins. "Damn, boys. I'm glad you're on our side!"

Cruz chuckles. "Yeah, well, not everyone appreciates our sense of protocol."

I strap on my vest. "If all goes well, we may need to talk about you two coming to work for my boss."

Ray nods in agreement. "Good call."

Once we are geared up, we set out toward the cabin. Joe and Cruz lead the way. Ray and I follow, weapons drawn, night vision goggles in place. A twig snapping on my left makes me stop in my tracks. A large shadow moves away from us.

Cruz taps my shoulder. "Bear," he whispers and walks away.

Bears. Just fucking great.

I catch up to the rest of the group. My heart speeds up when I see a light in the distance. I want to run, but Joe grabs my arm and shakes his head. He points to the windows in the back of the cabin. They are dark. We sneak up to the cabin to make sure Gina isn't in there. Cruz checks the window and clears what looked like a bathroom. Ray gives the all-clear for the bedroom. Gina and Tommy are together in the front room.

Damn it.

I was hoping we will be able to get Gina out without her being part of taking Tommy down. The four of us sneak around to the front of the cabin. My blood runs cold. Tommy is screaming at someone named Melissa. Does Tommy have an accomplice?

Shit.

I crouch low along the outside of the cabin and look in the small window. Tommy paces the room in an agitated state, waving a Glock 21 SF military issue. I know that gun—the clip held thirteen rounds.

I don't see Gina in the room, but then she speaks and my heart dropped. She speaks in low tones. He calls her Melissa. Tommy paces some more. I give the group the signal. Cruz kicks in the door, releasing the flash bomb.

GINA

All hell breaks loose.

The front door bursts open and a small canister rolls into the room. A second later, the room explodes in a burst of light and smoke. Tommy grabs me around the waist.

"Insurgents!" He puts the switchblade to my throat firing off rounds into the smoke. The smoke fills my lungs, making me cough. The blade bites into my skin, but Tommy won't loosen his hold on me.

"Give it up, Tommy. You're surrounded."

My heart jumps. "Cole!"

The blade cuts further into my neck. "You told them?" Tommy shakes with rage. "Why, Melissa? Why would you do that?"

Out of the corner of my eye, I see four figures enter the room in a low crouch.

“Tommy, I didn’t tell them. You have to believe me.”

“I won’t let them take you away from me again, Melissa. We are going to be together forever.” The blade cuts deeper into my throat. I taste blood.

“Tommy, no!”

A shot rings out. Something warm and wet covers my face. Tommy falls away from me and I look down.

There is a black hole where his left eye is supposed to be. A large pool of blood and grey stuff forms under his head. I reach up and feel my face; it is warm and sticky. I pull my hand back, it is covered in blood. My eyes flutter. My knees give out.

Cole reaches for me. “Gina!”

***

I open my eyes. It is dark. I am home. My throat hurts. I touch a thick bandage that covering my neck. Memories of Nick and Tommy flood my mind. It's too much. I close my eyes.

"How long is she going to be like this?"

"Vince, she's been through a series of traumatic events and needs to heal. I don't know how long that's going to take. She's in shock."

"Walt, I don't like it. It's been four days already. The doctor said she needs fluids, but she won't eat or drink anything."

I can't open my eyes. I don't want to face anyone yet, so I pretend to be asleep and listen.

"I'll have him put in an IV so she can stay hydrated."

My father sighs. "Alright."

The voices drift away. I feel a slight prick in my arm and fall back to sleep.

I know my family is worried. They all come and sit with me. Marco brushes my hair while James holds my hand, but I refuse to come back. Every night Cole curls around me. He whispers that he loves me and needs me to come back to him. Silent tears slip from my eyes. Cole kisses each one away.

COLE

This last week has been absolute hell. After we got Gina out of the cabin and had her neck tended to, she went into total shock and shut down. Her body is being kept hydrated through an IV. She hasn't opened her eyes in five days, but I know she's in there. Her tears tell me she's afraid. I need her to fight. I need her to come back to me. I need . . . .

"Is there coffee?"

I jump, ripped from my thoughts. There she is, my Gina.

She had showered and put on fresh clothes. They seem a little baggier than they did before. There is a bandage on her arm where her IV used to be and a new dressing on her neck. Her hollowed cheeks and pallid complexion make my heart ache.

Her eyes search every corner of the room. I'm not sure if she is going to stay or run back to her room.

I stand and take a step toward her. My heart breaks when she steps back. I hold my hands up and also step back. “Have a seat on the couch and I’ll get you something to eat.”

She nods, but doesn't move until I am out of the room.

When I come back in carrying a glass of juice and a plate of crackers, Gina had tucked herself into the furthest corner of the couch. She covers herself from chin to toe with a blanket. I keep the coffee table between us, but Gina shrinks back when I lean forward to put the plate down.

“Thank you,” she whispers, but doesn't touch anything until I sit at the dining table, putting some distance between us. She tentatively takes a sip of the juice and nibbles a cracker. She won't look at me.

“Gina?”

She jumps and shakes as if she forgot I am still in the room.

“Sweetheart, do you want me to leave? Do you want your mom or Abby here instead?”

A tear slides from her eye. “I want my mom.”

My stomach falls to my feet. “Alright.” I pull out my cell and call Ava.

The family is spending most of their time downstairs. They don't want to be too far away when Gina finally wakes up. Ava is in the apartment in a matter of seconds. Gina sees her mother and both burst into tears. Ava wraps her arms around Gina and croons to her in Italian about how grateful she is that her baby is alive and came back to them.

I feel like I am intruding and slip out the door unnoticed.

I get to my car and Vince is waiting for me. He looks up to the apartment windows. “How is she?”

I know it is killing him not to be up there with his daughter. Hell it's killing me not to be up there with his daughter. "She's up and showered, but still afraid."

Vince sighs. "Ava will get through to her." He looks me over. "You look like shit."

"So do you."

He claps me on the shoulder. "C'mon, let's get a drink."

Vince leads me to his car after taking one last look up at the apartment windows and saying a silent prayer.

GINA

It feels so good to have my mom with me. Cole is just too much for me to handle.

“He loves you so much.”

Mom sets a bowl of chicken broth in front of me. “He wouldn’t leave your side the entire time. He went with you in the ambulance and camped out on that stupid bean bag chair in your room. Even if one of us came in to sit with you, he wouldn’t leave. You had terrible nightmares the first few nights and he would gather you up in is arms and rock you. Abby and I couldn’t come within five feet of you when that happened. He threatened Ray and your father with bodily harm if they tried to take you from him. Even Carina didn’t scare him. He feels responsible for what happened to you.” Mom slides the spoon in the broth and holds it out to me.

I open my mouth to accept the broth. “It’s not his fault. It’s mine.”

The bowl clatters on the coffee table, broth sloshes over the sides and lands on the table. Mom is pissed.

“Gina Lucia Toriello!”

Shit. She triple named me. I am in for it now.

The woman, who is usually the voice of reason, stands and paces the room. “You are not responsible for Nick or Tommy’s death! Tommy was a deeply disturbed and broken man. No one could save him. His father is moving to Arizona and leaving Chester Springs because he is so ashamed.”

I gasp. “It’s not his fault.”

Mom stops pacing. “The guilt is eating him alive. He feels responsible for what happened. He said that Tommy took his meds when his father told him to, but when he left, Tommy stopped taking them. He feels if he stayed, none of this would have happened.”

I stand and grab my sneakers.

"Gina, what are you doing?"

"I need to see Mr. Reynolds, Mom. Can you take me?"

She smiles. "Let's go."

A few minutes later, we pull into the Reynolds' driveway. A *For Sale* sign stands in the front lawn and my heart breaks for Mr. Reynolds. His family name will always be associated with Nick's death.

I square my shoulders and knock on the door. Mr. Reynolds gasps when he sees me.

"Gina?"

I smile. "Hi, Mr. Reynolds. Can we talk to you for a minute?"

He takes a step back and holds the door open. Mom and I step into the living room. Several boxes are already packed.

"Please, sit. I'm surprised you're here. Gina, I can't even begin to tell you how sorry I am about what happened to you. Tommy . . . ." He coughs and when he sees my neck, his eyes get glassy.

I stand and hug him. At first, he is stiff, then his arms wrap around my back. He sobs into my hair. "I'm so sorry."

I let him cry for a few more minutes before I sit back down. Mr. Reynolds sits in a chair facing me.

"Who was Melissa?"

His eyes swing to mine. "What?"

Mom grabs my hand.

"Tommy kept calling me Melissa. From what I figured out, he loved her very much and she died when his unit was attacked?"

Mr. Reynolds hangs his head. "Melissa was Tommy's fiancée. It was her last tour. They were supposed to get married this Christmas. Three days before they were ambushed, Tommy called to tell me that Melissa was pregnant."

I grip mom's hand. "Oh my God."

Mr. Reynolds looks me in the eye. "She wasn't supposed to be out that night. They hadn't told their CO that Melissa was pregnant and she insisted on going with the unit. She and Tommy had a terrible fight about it. When she died, he just cracked. When he was recovering in Germany, he became obsessed with finding Melissa."

"Mr. Reynolds, what do you mean finding Melissa?"

"They didn't find her body with the rest of the unit. The assumption was she wasn't dead and the rebels took her."

Mom sobs. "That poor girl."

My hands tremble. "Did they ever find her?"

Mr. Reynolds nods. "Four days later. She had been brutally raped and beaten. She lost the baby. Her head was almost cut all the way off." He stands and leaves the room.

"My God, Mom," I whisper.

She wraps her arm around me and squeezes. “I know, baby. I know. Poor Tommy.”

Mr. Reynolds comes back into the room holding a framed photograph. “This was Melissa.” He holds the picture out to me. I gasp.

“She looks—”

“Just like you. I know.”

Melissa could have been our relative. Her long dark hair and deep brown eyes mirror mine. Her smile and facial features aren't exact, but strikingly similar.

“I was nervous when he started working for Ray, but then he seemed so much better. Now I see it was because he thought you were Melissa. I’m so sorry, Gina. Nick’s blood is on my hands, too.”

I stand and grab his hands. “Mr. Reynolds, it’s not your fault. You thought he was getting better. None of us saw what was really happening.”

I look at Mom. “It isn’t my fault, either.”

She smiles and stands. “Mr. Reynolds, I’m so sorry for what happened to Tommy. He was a good boy who broke under the weight of his guilt. Please don’t let that happen to you as well. We don’t hold you responsible for what happened to Gina. I’m sure the Zacco’s feel the same way.”

He nods. “Nick’s brother called yesterday and told me that. He said that while Nick’s death was a tragedy, what happened to Tommy was also a tragedy and he wasn’t in his right frame of mind. He spoke of forgiveness, not hatred.”

My mother embraces Mr. Reynolds briefly and stands back. “I understand why you want to go to Arizona, but please know that if you ever want to come back, we will welcome you.”

With glassy eyes, Mr. Reynolds opens the front door. “Thank you both so much.”

My mom and I get into the car. We drive for a few minutes before she speaks.

"That was a very brave thing you did. I know Mr. Reynolds is grateful for your forgiveness, Gina, but I'm curious. Did you mean what you said about Nick and Tommy's death's not being your fault either?"

I take a deep breath and let it out slowly. "I think so, Mom."

She smiles and pats my knee, turning the car into the restaurant parking lot. "Welcome back, Gina."

COLE

I tip back the scotch, feeling the burn slide down my throat. I am surrounded by the men in Gina's family. Vince sits to my right, Ray to my left, and Max is across from me. We sit around Max's kitchen table.

"Cole, I can't thank you enough for saving my daughter."

I nod and take another sip of scotch. It doesn't matter that I saved Gina. I am going to lose her all over again.

Max gets my attention. "She'll come around, man. You'll see."

I nod again. Abby buzzes into the room and puts down a plate of food. I don't even notice what is on it. Her slender arms circle my shoulders. She gives me a squeeze. "I'm happy you all made it out of there alright. But if you ever scare us like that again . . . ." She gives me another squeeze.

"I know, you'll kick my ass with your pretty little black belt."

She stands and huffs. "Pretty little black belt?"

Max groans and pulls her into his lap. "Easy, tiger. Cole's just trying to get a rise out of you. His own woman won't fight with him; you're the closest thing he's got."

I snort, taking another sip of my drink.

"Aww, Cole. That's sweet. I'd totally kick your ass, but sweet."

I snort again. "Sure you would, honey."

Max shakes his head. "Babe? No."

But it is too late. I pissed off Abby. "Let's go, Cole. Me and you, in the yard, right fucking now. I know you saved Gina and I'll be forever grateful for that, but you do not get to come in my house and insult me, got it?" She takes off her shoes and stomps toward the back door. "Let's go, asshole."

Max groans again. “Dude, what the fuck? We were having a nice time.” He looks at Ray. “Why does she have to kick everyone’s ass?”

“Let it go, Max.” Vince winks at me. “He made his bed.”

I down the last of the amber liquid and stand. “This should be fun.” I take two steps and stop. “If I kick your wife’s ass, are you gonna kick mine?”

While I am military trained for hand to hand combat, Max is still a big guy.

Max smirks. “If you win no, but I doubt you will.” Ray and Vince nod in agreement.

Great, now I have to kick a woman’s ass because my man card is on the line. What the hell kind of mess did I get myself into?

I walk out into the yard. Abby is warming up. She looks pretty good, too. Maybe I underestimated her skills.

Shit.

Abby bounces on the balls of her feet like a boxer. “Ready, asshole?” She smirks and blows Max a kiss.

I look over my shoulder. All three men have the same stance. Arms crossed over their chests, smirks tugging their lips. They wait for me to make the next move.

I crack my neck. “Let’s go, Mary Poppins.”

My insult has the desired effect. Abby lowers herself into a crouch and waits. I dance around, sizing her up. She is sharp. Her eyes never leaving mine. Deciding it will be best to make the first move and get this over with, I lunge and try to sweep her legs, but Abby is quicker than I expect. She springs up like a cat. Her foot connects with my face. I grunt and take a step back. She lands quietly on her feet and assumes an attack position.

“Lucky shot, Abby. You won’t get another one.”

She smirks and waggles her eyebrows.

I try waiting her out, but she is smart and very well trained. I have to congratulate Walt on his star pupil the next time I see him.

Abby straightens. “I guess you don’t know how to fight very well.”

She makes the mistake of turning her back on me. I make my move. I take one step before I feel my legs go out from under me. Abby’s foot presses on my throat. “Give up yet?”

Fuck she is good. I walked right into her little trap.

I grab her foot with both hands and push. Using my own power against me, Abby’s other foot steps on my chest as she somersaults mid- air and comes down like a cat. I stand up.

“Not bad, Cole. Most men tap out when I do that move.”

“I’m not most men.”

I engage Abby in hand to hand combat. She meets me blow for blow. She is in great shape and doesn't seem to tire. My lungs scream in protest, but I am not ready to give up. I try one last move, but am once again on my back. I tap the ground twice and close my eyes. I lost.

Abby stands over me, extending her hand to help me up. "I have a feeling if your lungs were completely healed, this may have ended differently."

I grunt. "I doubt it. Walt taught you well."

Abby puts her hands at her sides and bows. It is a sign of respect. I return the gesture.

Abby smiles as Max kisses the top of her head. "So Cole, now that Abby's gotten you out of your funk, are you ready to go fight for your own woman?"

I mirror all of their smiling faces. "Hell yes."

Vince chuckles. "Ava texted me that she and Gina went out for a bit, but they're home and Gina wants to see you.

My heart swells. "Let's go."

GINA

Mom checks her phone. “They’re on their way.”

I am nervous. Mom gives me a reassuring squeeze and smiles. “It’ll be fine, baby. Just speak from your heart.”

“Thanks, Mom.”

She smiles and leaves to wait for my dad downstairs.

After speaking to Mr. Reynolds, a huge weight has been lifted from my shoulders. I want to be with Cole. I love him. It is time he knew that.

I walk into my bedroom and stop. Mom had changed the sheets; put the beanbag chair in the closet. She knows seeing that chair will remind Cole what happened.

Damn, my mom is awesome.

I spritz on perfume and brush out my hair until it falls in soft waves down my back. My clothes are a little baggier, but there is nothing I can do to change that right now.

I go into the kitchen and pull out a bottle of tequila. I need a shot of liquid courage. After slamming two shots, there is a knock on the door.

“Gina? It’s Cole. Can I come in?”

He is asking permission. This man who is usually in control asks for my permission.

“Come in.”

He takes a step in and closes the door behind him, but comes no further into the apartment. He looks exhausted. Dark circles rimd his eyes. The stubble on his jaw is thick and dark. There is a fresh bruise forming on his cheek.

I step to him, but he doesn't move. I reach out and stroke his cheek. He closes his eyes and nuzzles my hand.

“What happened to your face?”

Cole smirks. “Abby kicked my ass.”

“She what?” Cole gently grabs my wrist, keeping my hand on his face.

“It’s fine. Don’t leave me, Gina. Please.” His eyes are pained.

“Oh, Cole. What have I done to you?” A tear slides down my face. Cole bends to kiss it away.

“You’ve stolen my heart, Gina. I love you. Please don’t leave me again.”

I shake my head. “I won’t. I promise. I love you, too, Cole.”

“I thought I’d lost you forever.”

“Not forever. I’m back now and I’m not going anywhere.”

He smiles. “Thank Christ.”

His mouth crashes down over mine. I curl into him and moan as his hands travel down my back and cup my ass.

He lifts me and my legs wrap around his waist. Cole pulls back, his breathing ragged. “Gina?” He is again asking for my permission.

I kiss along his jaw and gently bite his earlobe, Cole to moans my name. “Take me to bed, Cole.”

He crosses the living room, not putting me down, and kicks open my bedroom door. He gently lays me down on the bed, kissing my neck. “Oh, Gina. What you do to me.”

His erection digs into my hip and I wiggle under him. He looks at me, pupils dilating. “I want to be sweet to you, Gina, but if you do that again, I won’t be able to.”

I wiggle and smirk. “Cole, I’m not a china doll. I don’t want sweet or slow. I need you to fuck me hard and fast. Please, Cole. Help me forget.”

He kisses me; his hands grip the collar of my t-shirt as his tongue plunges into my mouth. My shirt rips down the front. My nipples harden as moisture pools between my thighs. Cole unhooks my bra. In an instant, his tongue swirls my nipples into hardened points. My hands fist in his hair. I pull as Cole bit down. My hips buck under him. Cole groans as his hands travel down. Soon my pants and underwear are on the floor. His fingers stroke me.

"Fuck, Gina."

I reach down and try to undo his jeans. I let out a frustrated groan. "Off. Now."

Cole chuckles. "Patience baby."

I shake my head. "No. Off now. I want to feel your skin on mine."

Cole stands. I crawl up the bed as his jeans slide to the floor. His erection is simply magnificent. It jerks under my heated gaze and I lick my lips. Cole lets out a groan as he steps out of his pants.

"Condom?"

Cole reaches for his wallet and fishes out the foil packet. He rips it open with his teeth. I scurry to the end of the bed. "Wait."

I grab the opened packet and put it on the bed.

"Gina?"

I want to taste him, all of him. Swiping my tongue over the tip of Cole's straining erection, he hisses. "Baby."

I suck him deeper into my mouth, hollowing my cheeks as I slide over him. It is hard and soft. He tastes divine. Cole stiffens as he stands. "Baby, I don't want to come like this."

I am not listening to him. I need to, and I *want* to, do this. I continue sliding my mouth and tongue over his length. My hand gently cups and massages his balls.

"Gina . . . I can't—fuck!" His release hits the back of my throat. It tastes thick and salty. It isn't as bad as I thought it would be; in fact I like it. I continue to coax every last drop from Cole's spent body. When I am finished, I release him with a wet pop.

Cole flops back on the bed, his breathing ragged. "Why did you do that? I wanted to make you feel good, first."

I trace my fingers over the ridges on his abdomen. “I wanted to. I've never done that before.”

Cole leans up on his elbows. “Given a blowjob?”

I sigh. “No. I’ve never . . . swallowed before.”

Cole’s eyebrows shoot up. “Really? Never?”

I shake my head. “Nope. I always thought it would be gross. Abby said she never did until she was with Max and now she likes to do it.”

Cole looks me in the eye. “And how do you feel about it now?”

I grin. “I wanna do it again.”

Cole collapses on the bed, laughing. “Baby, I need a few minutes to recover, but I can do something for you while we wait.”

I give him a coy smile. “Oh?”

Cole springs up and pushes me back. His body covers mine as he presses kisses on my throat. He hits the spot below my ear, making me shudder.

"Oh."

Cole's hands roam over me; one gently kneads my breast while the other travels lower. Cole kisses his way down my body until he settles between my thighs. He opens my legs, planting kisses up and down my thighs, purposefully avoiding my center.

I wiggle and groan. "Cole, please."

He chuckles. "I'm going to have to teach you some patience, baby." He kisses my thighs again. "I can smell how much you want me, Gina, but how do you taste?" He runs his tongue over my folds.

I buck under his mouth. "Oh God, Cole."

Cole's mouth is replaced with two long fingers. He pumps in and out of me as his tongue swirls over my clit.

"Holy shit!" The orgasm rips through me. It feels like Cole is reaching into my soul.

The crinkle of the condom wrapper makes me open eyes long enough to watch him plunge into me. I cry out from the sheer size and length of him.

Cole stills. "Shit, Gina. I'm sorry. I should have gone slower to get you used to me, but I just couldn't wait."

I take a deep breath and relax while my body adjusts. I shift and swear he gets thicker. Cole's eyes are closed.

.

Once he is completely seated, I need him to move. Clenching my inner walls around him, his eyes snap open. "Gina." His tone is a warning.

"Yes?"

I clench again and smirk when Cole hisses. He pulls out almost all the way before plunging back into me. I cry out, my nails raking down his back.

Cole grunts and picks up the pace. My orgasm hits me like a freight train. After a few more thrusts, Cole's release follows. He falls on top of me. I wrap my arms and legs around him, keeping him in place. Even after he goes soft, I won't let go. Cole shifts and slips out of me. He goes to the bathroom to dispose of the condom. He returns a minute later and tucks us into bed. I curl into him and draw lazy circles on his smooth chest. His hand strokes my back.

"I thought I'd never see you again."

Cole's hand stills. "I was afraid of the same thing, baby, but you played it smart."

I frown. "I did?"

He nods. "You kept him talking. I heard you. You didn't raise your voice or freak out. You were calm, so he was calm."

"I figured it was the only way to stay alive."

Cole kisses my temple. "My smart girl. Sleep now, baby."

Wrapping my arm around his waist, I fall asleep with Cole stroking my back.

COLE

Today I got the call I have been dreading.

“Cole, the threat has been eliminated. I need you here.”

I sigh. Walt needs me to go to London. I am supposed to train the new operatives before running the new office. The problem is, I am in love with Gina and didn’t want to leave her. I need an administrative assistant and Walt gave me carte blanche to hire whomever I want. I am afraid Gina won't leave her family.

“Hey, are you alright?”

I look up from the newspaper I am not reading. There is concern in Gina’s eyes.

“I’m fine.”

She narrows her eyes while reaching for my coffee. I love how comfortable we have become with each other.

“I’m calling bullshit, Cole. You weren’t even looking at the paper and you had a scowl on your face. What’s going on?”

I sigh and put down the paper. “Walt called this morning.”

Gina sits at the table. “Yeah, so?”

I give her a pointed look. “The threat against you has been eliminated.”

She nods and sips my coffee. “Uh huh . . . . Oh.” Recognition flashes in her eyes. “You have to go.”

I nod. “I have to go.”

She pushes the cup away and bends her head, her hair forming a curtain around her face. “When?”

“Walt wanted me to leave today, but I told him you still needed me, so he gave me until the end of the week.”

Her shoulders shake with silent sobs. My heart breaks to see her in pain. “So we have four days?”

“Gina, look at me, please.”

She stands and turns from the table. "I need a shower."

She bolts from the room. I rise to go after her, but she locks the bathroom door. Sitting outside the door listening to her cry completely shatters me.

A little while later, Gina comes out wrapped in a fluffy blue towel. I sit on the edge of the bed, my forearms resting on my knees.

Gina's eyes are red and puffy, but she plasters on a smile for me. "What do you want to do today?"

I stand. "I think we need to talk about this."

She shakes her head. "No. I want to do something fun. Maybe take a drive to the Jersey shore?"

"Gina."

"It's off season. Maybe we could stay overnight."

She goes into her closet, comes out with a small duffel and starts packing. "I mean, I know it's too cold to go swimming, but maybe we could sit on the beach and watch the waves? Or maybe go to Atlantic City if you want to do some gambling." She haphazardly piles clothes into the bag.

I grab her hands. "Gina, stop. Talk to me."

She tries to shake free, but I tighten my grip.

"Cole, I don't know what you want to talk about. You're leaving me in four days."

I throw the duffel on the floor, sat on the bed and pull Gina on my lap. "Baby, you know I don't want to leave you, right?"

She shrugs and won't look at me.

I grasp her chin, locking her eyes on mine. "I. Love. You. I don't want to leave you; you have to know that."

"I don't want you to go, Cole. Can't you stay?"

I shake my head. "I wish I could, Gina, but Walt needs me in London."

She looks at her lap. "When will you be back?"

“Walt wants me to run the offices over there. I don’t know that I would be coming back.”

“Oh,” she whispers. Tears slides over her nose and drips onto her hands.

“You could come with me.”

Gina’s head jerks up. “What?”

I smile. “I said, you could come with me. I need a personal assistant and Walt said I could hire anyone I wanted. I want you.”

Her smile slips. “Y--you want me because of my managerial skills?”

I chuckle. “I want you because I love you. The thought of you being so far away instead of in my arms where you belong pisses me off. Your office skills are a bonus.”

Gina’s smile melts my heart. “I want to go.”

I am shocked. “Seriously? Gina, I want you to think about this. The work we’ll be doing is strictly confidential. You can't tell anyone about our clients or what we do. No one, Gina. Not even your family."

She rolls her eyes. "Well, duh. I know that."

I look her in the eyes. "Do you think you could live in London and not see your family every day?"

She doesn't move. "Can they visit us? I mean, as long as we don't bring them to the office?"

I smile. "Of course they can."

"I can set my mom up with a Skype account, too, right?"

I kiss the tip of her nose. "Anything you want, baby."

She grins, bounces off my lap, and lets out a whoop. "Holy shit. We're going to London!"

I pick her up and spin her around before kissing her deeply. "We're going to London."

GINA

"Oh, shit."

Cole sits back down, pulling me onto his lap. "What's wrong?"

"My family is going to freak out."

He kisses my nose. "It'll be fine."

I jump off his lap and pace the room. "There's no way on God's green Earth my father will approve of me moving to London and shacking up with you."

Cole chuckles. I glare at him.

"Oh come on, Gina! He does realize you're an adult, right?"

I shake my head. "You don't understand. My family is very traditional. If we were married, then it would be different."

The color drains from his face. “Shit, Cole. Breathe! I’m not saying we need to get married.” Although his reaction scares me a little. I don't want to be with another man who says he loves me, but doesn't want to marry me.

He lets out a breath, some color returning to his cheeks. “Baby, it’s not that I don’t want to marry you . . . someday.”

I am so relieved, I start to laugh. “I get it. I do. Now we have to convince my dad and Uncle Ray.”

He stands. “I’ll go talk to them.”

I beam. “As much as I love you for saying that, we’ll go together.”

***

“No.”

“Daddy—”

“Absolutely not. You are not going half way around the world to live with some man who isn’t even your husband! What if things don’t work out? What will you do then?”

I flinch as if he struck me. “Are you saying, if I go to London with Cole, I can’t ever come home?”

Dad looks at Uncle Ray and then Mom. My mother narrows her eyes and points at him. “Choose your next words wisely, Vince.” Uncle Ray nods in silent agreement.

Dad runs a hand down his face and sighs. “Of course not. You will always have a home here.” He speaks to me while staring at Cole.

Cole stiffens slightly, but nods.

I throw my arms around my father’s neck, planting a sloppy kiss on his cheek. “You know you’ll always be the first man I ever loved, right,” I whisper in his ear.

He squeezes my arms and sighs. “Be careful in London.”

I squeal and hug Mom. Her eyes are glassy, but she laughs. “Go and be happy, Bella.”

Uncle Ray stands and hugs me as well before he rounds on Cole. “I’ve seen how much you love her, but remember, we love her too. If you hurt her, God himself won’t be able to find you after I do.”

I stiffen, but smile when Uncle Ray whispers in my ear, “He’s a good man, but a little fear is healthy.”

Cole is a little pale. I wind my way out of my uncle’s embrace and leap into Cole’s arms. “I guess I’m going to London with you.”

He smirks and whispers, “I never had any doubt.”

COLE

"Baby, you know they have stores in London, right?"

I look around Gina's apartment and sigh. She insists on taking almost everything she owns. There are several boxes already on their way to London and now she is packing all her "essentials." We are leaving tomorrow. All I want is her naked and screaming my name, not dealing with her clothes.

She huffs. "Cole, I need my clothes. Geez, if it were up to you, I'd wear nothing all day." She smirks and wags her eyebrows.

She is right. I love having her naked and in my arms. It is my new addiction. "Damn right."

"Well, that might be a little awkward in the office, don't you think?"

I growl at the thought of any man besides me seeing her naked and walk into the closet, pulling out everything that is left. “Here. Pack these, too.”

Gina laughs, taking the clothes from my arms. “Aw, baby. So, no naked office time?”

I sweep her up in my arms, kissing her deeply. “The only naked time will be in my *private* office behind locked doors.”

She squirms. My eyes narrow. “You’re thinking about it right now, aren’t you?”

“No.”

I chuckles. “Oh, baby. You’re a terrible liar.”

She wiggles out of my embrace. “Alright, mister. I need to finish packing if we’re going to leave on time tomorrow.”

I grab the clothes and throw them aside. “They can wait.” I pulled the suitcase on the bed to the floor. Gina squeals and takes off into the living room. I chuckle, stalking after her.

It doesn't take long to catch her; the apartment isn't that big. She is in the kitchen hiding in a corner when I spot her.

"Seriously? Baby, don't you know I'll always find you?"

She stands and smirks. "Well now that you've caught me, whatever will you do with me?" She bats her eyelashes.

I stalk closer. Her breathing picks up. Good. I love to build the anticipation for her. I reach behind her head as she closes her eyes. Opening the cabinet and pulling out a glass, I chuckle as Gina huffs a frustrated sigh.

When my glass is full of water from the sink, I turn and sip. "Thirsty?" I offer her the glass. She watches me, shakes her head. I shrug. "Suit yourself." I turn back to put the glass in the sink, catching Gina around the waist when she tries to leave the kitchen.

"Where do you think you're going?"

"To finish packing."

"Oh, no. Not yet." I lift her and place her on the kitchen countertop. I nudge between her legs, placing a hand on either side of her thighs. "I'm feeling a little peckish and wanted a snack. Do you mind?"

Gina shrugs.

"Good."

I lean in and capture her mouth with mine. A soft moan escapes from her lips. I get half hard from one sound. I run my tongue along her lips, demanding entrance. Gina opens for me and I stroke her tongue with my own. Her hands run through my hair and down my back. She wiggles to the edge of the countertop, pressing into my erection. I hiss as she runs her nails up my back, taking my shirt off. We stop kissing long enough for our shirts to fly across the room. Then her mouth is back on mine. I unclasp her bra, throwing it down. Her hard nipples brush against my chest. I hiss again. This woman has the power to unman me with the simple touch of her skin on mine.

"Cole," she whispers.

I can't wait another second. I yank her pants and underwear down. I part her slick folds with my fingers and thrust out my tongue. Gina lays back on the countertop and moans. I swipe my tongue over her clit. She writhes.

"You taste amazing."

"Cole," She moans. "Stop teasing me."

That is all I need to hear. Sucking, licking and nipping at every inch of her core makes Gina bow off the countertop.

"So…close…oh…fuck!"

Gina comes and I lap up every drop.

"Oh Cole…" Gina's body shakes on the countertop.

God, I love hearing my name on her lips. I grab her around the waist, lifting her. Gina's legs wrap around my waist as I carry her to the closest bedroom. I gently lay Gina down on the comforter, my body covering hers. I kiss along her jaw, hitting the spot below her ear I know makes her crazy. I suck gently on her neck. She squirms under me.

"Cole, please."

I work my way down to her tight, dusky nipples. I swirl my tongue around one, massaging the other with my hand. Gina arches, letting me take her breast deeper in my mouth. She moans as I gently bite down on one nipple while pinching the other.

I recently discovered my girl enjoys a little pain with her pleasure. I can't wait to explore that once we get to London.

Gina reaches for my jeans, working them open.

I chuckle. "Always so eager."

She opens her eyes. "Cole, please. I need you."

"I know what you need, baby. Hang on," I say while trying to work my jeans and boxers off. Apparently I am taking too long. One minute Gina is lying on the bed, the next minute, Gina is off the bed, yanking off my jeans and boxers. She stands before me, naked with fire in her eyes, her hands on her curvy hips. “Lay down on the bed.”

I arch an eyebrow. “Excuse me?”

She points to the bed. “You. On your back. Now.”

I comply. Gina usually gives me control in the bedroom, but this side of her is fucking hot.

When I am situated the way she wanted, Gina smiles. “Good boy.”

“Watch it, Gina.”

She saunters over to the bed. Her tongue darts out and licks her lips before she sucks her bottom lip between her teeth. My cock jumps. Gina smiles.

She reaches the bed, pushing my ankles apart. Gina rakes her nails up my calves then down my thighs. I gasp, my cock jumping again. A second later, soft kisses replace her nails. I sink deeper into the mattress, closing my eyes. God, this woman is going to kill me.

The bed dips. A warm wet tongue skates across my abdomen and over my hips. I groan, lifting my hips to meet her mouth.

Gina chuckles. “Now who’s eager?”

Her nose brushes over my balls. I almost spring off the bed. A second later, her tongue swirles over my sac and my balls tighten. I fist the sheets when she gently takes one of my balls into her hot, wet mouth and sucks.

“Oh, God, Gina. Are you trying to kill me?” She has never done this before. I almost blow my load right there.

She doesn't answer; instead the tip of her tongue works its way up my hard shaft. When her tongue flattens and she licks me like an ice cream cone, I take back control. Gina’s eyes widen as I grab her waist and flip her onto her back.

“Baby, as much as I fucking loved what you were doing to me, I want to be inside you when I come.”

Gina grabs my hair as her lips crash onto mine. I reach down and find her already so wet.

"Damn, baby. That's so fucking hot."

"Cole, stop talking and fuck me already."

I line up and enter her with one swift thrust. Gina arches her back as I capture her breast with my mouth. She moans as I continue to suck and bite her nipples.

"Oh, God, Cole. That feels amazing." I pick up my pace and reach down to stroke her clit. Gina's inner muscles clench around me. I pound her with a force I never knew I had.

She is close. I won't be able to hold on much longer. I pull almost all the way out and pinch her clit as I thrust back in. Gina screams my name, convulsing around me. Two thrusts later, my own release empties into her.

Three days ago when Gina told me she was on birth control and wanted me to fuck her bareback, I was amazed. Now I am addicted to her. I've never done this with another woman before. She is it. My one.

I pull out. My release runs down her thigh. I almost stand and beat my chest. A satisfied smile crosses my lips as I think about how this amazing woman is all mine.

“What are you smiling about?”

Gina’s eyes are half open. Her hair has that sexy just-fucked look. She is perfect.

“I was just smiling about how amazing you are.”

She blushes. "You make me feel that way.”

I kiss her nose. “Don’t move.” I walk into the bathroom and wet a washcloth with warm water. Gina was surprised the first time I cleaned her up after we had sex. It makes me wonder what kind of men she was with before if the simple act of caring for her is a surprise. It pisses me off that no one took the time to care for Gina the way she deserves. I shake my head. That is all in the past. She is mine now and I take care of what’s mine.

GINA

I can't believe we are finally here. London is beautiful. After assuring everyone in my family that I am fine, Cole and I christen every room in our new flat.

I am getting dressed for my first day as the personal assistant to one of the sexiest, smartest men I have ever known.

"Baby, are you ready?" Cole walks into the bedroom and stops.

He looks amazing in a suit. The charcoal gray suit with the new periwinkle shirt I got him before we left makes my mouth water. His broad shoulders fit perfectly in the jacket and the slight five o'clock shadow makes him look even hotter. He holds out two ties, but when his eyes land on me, both fall from his hands and flutter to the floor.

"What the hell are you wearing?"

My eyes sweep downward. I think I look appropriate for a fancy office. The black pencil skirt goes to the top of my knees and the red silk blouse isn't too tight across my boobs. The red peep toe pumps match my blouse. I even put my hair up in a messy but stylish bun rather than leave it down. The damp weather in London is going to be hell on my thick hair. I feel better with it up.

"What's wrong with what I'm wearing?"

Cole slips off his suit jacket and puts it around my shoulders. It falls almost to my knees. "That's better."

I look down, roll my eyes, and shrug out of the coat, handing it back to him. "What is wrong with you?"

He stalks over to the closet and pulls out the shapeless caftan Marco bought me as a gag gift for Christmas. "Wear this."

I frown. "Cole, what's going on?" I take the caftan from his white knuckled grasp and hang it back in the closet.

“You look too damn sexy in that outfit. The thought of other men seeing you in that tight little skirt and those red fuck me heels pisses me off.”

I smile. My alpha male is protective.

“Cole, I love you. No one else can or will ever have me.” I bend over, pick up the ties from the floor, and hear Cole groan.

A pair of strong hands spin me around. “Don’t do that at work. In fact, I want you to sit at your desk and not move from there all day.”

I chuckle and hand him a tie. “I love you. You’re ridiculous, but I love you.”

COLE

If one more man looks at Gina with an appreciative smirk, I am going to get arrested. She isn't even aware of just how sexy she comes across. Our new flat is in a luxury complex complete with a doorman. He is the first guy I wanted to punch this morning. Then there is Nigel, the driver Walt sent to bring us to the office. He gives Gina a flirty wink as she slides into the back of the car. When he looks at me, the smile falls from his face. As soon as we pull away from the curb, Gina lean over and gives me a sweet, sensuous kiss. When she settles back into her seat, I meet Nigel's eyes in the rearview and arch an eyebrow. He gives me a slight nod and focuses his attention on the road ahead.

Take that, motherfucker.

"Are you done?" Gina whispers.

"What?"

She rolls her eyes. "If you piss on my leg to mark your territory and ruin my skirt I'm gonna be pissed."

Nigel coughs. Gina giggles.

"Relax Cole. I'm only interested in you."

"Whatever." I refuse to look at either of them for the rest of the ride.

When we get to the new office building, security has to check our credentials and takes us to have our pictures taken for our corporate ID's. It is just a card that gives us access to all parts of the complex. Each is embedded with a small microchip so employees can be tracked within the building, but the only ones who knows about that are Walt and I. Our thumbprints are scanned into the system. I explain to Gina that this is part of the security protocol. Thumbprints are what access all the doors and elevators in the complex. No keys are used. Keys can be lost or copied; Walt feels that fingerprint recognition is better.

Gina smiles. "Makes sense. I mean, you're never without your thumb, right?"

I chuckle. "Give it a try."

Gina's eyes widen when her thumb scans and the elevator speaks to her. "Good morning, Miss Toriello."

"Damn. That's like some cool James Bond shit right there!"

I laugh, lacing my fingers with Gina's as the doors open to our floor.

Gina looks around and frowns.

"What's wrong?"

She shrugs. "It looks like a regular office."

I shake my head. "As far as anyone is concerned, it is a regular office. We run a *security* company, remember?"

An older woman sits at the reception desk. "Good morning, Mr. Taylor, Miss Toriello. My name is Constance Plumb. Mr. Scott sends his apologies. He was called away for a meeting earlier this morning, but said he will see you soon."

I nod. "Thank you, Ms. Plumb."

She smiles. "Your offices are one floor up in suites marked *Bravo* and *Charlie*."

We thank her again before heading back to the elevator. Seconds later, we are walking down the hallway to our suites. There are only three offices on this floor—Walt has the suite marked *Alpha*, I have *Bravo,* and there is a smaller office with the word *Charlie* on it for Gina.

Gina reads the doors, chuckling as I open the door to my office. "You can take the boy out of the military, but…" The sentiment dies on her lips.

My eyes follow hers and the smile falls from my face as well.

"Hello, Cole."

"Fiona." My back straightens as I spit out her name.

I grip Gina's hand. Fiona sees the movement and raises a perfectly sculpted blonde eyebrow. She advances on Gina. I want to step between the women, but Gina lets go of me and steps forward, extending her hand. "Good morning, Fiona. I'm Gina, Cole's assistant."

Fiona sneers. “I’m Cole’s wife. It’s nice to meet you.”

Gina freezes, but quickly recovers. “Well, I’ll let you two talk. Fiona would you like some coffee or tea?”

“No. Please close the door behind you on your way out, Tina.”

Gina squares her shoulders. “It’s Gina.” She turns to face me, hurt in her eyes. I need to talk to her, explain everything. I take a step toward her, but stop when a small tear slips down her cheek.

“If you’ll excuse me, Mr. Taylor. I’ll be at my desk if you need anything.” She strides out of the office, slamming the door behind her.

I turn to face a smirking Fiona. “She’s lovely, Cole. Wherever did you find her?”

“How did you get in here, Fiona, and what the fuck do you want?”

Her smile fades. She sits on the couch. “Now is that anyway to greet your wife?”

"You have three minutes before I have you arrested for trespassing."

"Your assistant isn't your usual type, Cole. I'm surprised."

"Two minutes, Fiona."

She huffs. "Fine. I want you back, Cole. I miss you. I miss us."

I bark a laugh. "Are you fucking serious, Fiona? We posed as a married couple for twelve days as part of a *mission.* Our marriage wasn't real! I didn't love you then and I sure as shit don't love you now."

"Well it was real to me! I love you, damn it!" She stands. "You sure seemed to like me well enough when you fucked me on the yacht all night long."

I shrug. "There were cameras in our room; I had to make it look believable."

She flinches as if I struck her. "You're lying! You love me. I know you do."

"You need to get the fuck out of my office right now."

"That sounds like a good idea to me."

I spin around. Walt stands in the doorway with his arms crossed over his chest. Fiona visibly shrinks seeing him there.

"Walt, please let me explain—"

Walt pushes off the door frame and enters my office. Two armed guards follow him. Walt pins Fiona with a glare as he speaks to the men. "Please escort this woman home. I don't want to ever see her in this building again and if she makes an attempt to contact any member of my staff or tries to flee from you today, she is to be eliminated. Understand?"

Fiona sways as the color drains from her face. "You wouldn't!"

Walt's stare never wavers. "It's done. Goodbye, Fiona."

The guards advance, each grabbing her by an arm. They ware almost out the door when Walt stops them. "Consider yourself lucky that you get to leave this office at all today, Fiona. Don't cross me. You won't live to regret it."

She whimpers and hangs her head, but when she smiles at me, a shiver runs down my spine.

As soon as she is gone, Walt relaxes and gives me a pat on the back. "I'm still sorry I ever got involved with that crazy bitch." He looks around the room. "Where's Gina?"

"Shit. I need to talk to her."

Walt nods. "I'll be in my office if you need any backup." He winks.

GINA

Married? Of course he is married. I know it is too good to be true. Once again, I am being used by some man. God, when the hell will I learn? What's worse, now I am stuck in fucking London! I check the time. It is late in Pennsylvania, but I pick up my desk phone anyway.

"Hello?"

Shit. I woke her up.

"Abby?" I sob.

"Gina? What's going on? Are you alright?"

"H—he's m—m—married."

"He's married? What? Who's married, sweetie?"

Abby shifts around. I hear Max grunt.

"Cole's married. I just met his freaking gorgeous blonde wife. She's, like, runway beautiful. God, I'm so stupid."

"What the hell do you mean Cole's married?" Abby shrieks. There is more shuffling. "Max get your ass out of bed right now! Where are you Gina? I'm getting dressed and coming to get you right now. Max will charter a plane so we can get there faster, which is good because I want to kill that asshole right now!"

I laugh; I can't help it. I picture Abby throwing on clothes and charging the airport. She and Max will rescue me in a second if I let them.

"Abby, stop. I love you and Max so much, but I need to handle this myself. I think I just needed to hear your fire to spark my own."

The shuffling stops. "Are you sure? We can be there by dinner. Walt can help get rid of the body. Damn it! Why didn't he tell us Cole was married? You deal with Cole; I have a call to make. Call me if you need an alibi, to get rid the body, or bail money. I'm still offering a supreme ass kicking, too."

"I love you, Abby."

"Lei è incredibile e nessuno può prendere che da voi. Ti amo anch'io." *You are amazing and no one can take that from you. I love you, too.*

I brush a tear from the corner of my eye as I hang up the phone. A few seconds later, a phone rings down the hall and I smile. I want to feel bad for Walter—he is about to experience Abby's wrath—but if Cole really is married and he kept that from the family, then as far as I'm concerned, Walter deserves everything he is about to get.

Cole's married. He lied to me. He said he loved me.

I am seething. How dare he? I'm not some stupid little plaything. I'm no one's puttana! I kick off my heels and pace my office, cursing him in English and Italian.

"Damn, baby, do you really want to castrate me and hang my balls in the Tower of London?"

I stop. Cole stands in the doorway of my office. At least it is my office for about ten more minutes. There is no way in hell I am staying here with a lying, cheating, married bastard. I pick up one of my shoes and throw it at Cole's smug face.

“Ti odio! Come hai potuto mentirmi così? Hai detto che mi amavi! Sei un bugiardo, barare bastardo e io non sarò il vostro puttana!” *I hate you! How could you lie to me like that? You said you loved me! You're a lying, cheating bastard and I won't be your whore!*

He crosses the room in two strides, pinning me against the wall. His hands grip my upper arms roughly. I know I’ll be bruised tomorrow, but don't care. I flail out a leg to kick him, but he easily blocks it.

“Non ho mai mentito maledizione. Ti amo! Fiona era mia moglie come parte di una missione. Non era vero o giuridica. E se mai riferimento a se stessi come una puttana di nuovo ti sculacciare voi fino a quando il culo perfetto si illumina di rosso. Mi capisci?”

I never lied to you, damn it. I love you! Fiona was my wife as part of a mission. It wasn't real or legal. And if you ever refer to yourself as a whore again, I will spank you until your perfect ass glows red. Do you understand me?

I nod. Cole lets me go. I rub my arms.

“Did I hurt you?” The concern in Cole’s voice melts my heart a little.

“I’m fine. Explain everything to me, please. Right now.”

Cole sighs and sits in one of the chairs facing my desk. I sit behind the desk, needing a little distance for the moment.

“Fiona was brought in by Walt about a year after I was. She was part of the CIA as a languages expert and was deciphering military chatter when she heard a plan between two rebel groups. They wanted to kidnap a rival leader’s ten year old daughter and sell her as a sex slave.”

I gasp. “Oh my God.”

Cole nods. “Walt still has connections in the CIA. His connection knew Walt worked with this particular leader before and gave him a call. Fiona was sent as an operative of the CIA to assist us. She was able to interpret the communications between the rebels. Walt sent us to keep an eye on the girl. Fiona’s cover was she was to be the girl’s governess and I was to be her

English tutor. Fiona and I posed as husband and wife so I had access to the girl and the grounds at all times without raising suspicion. We were flown in and asumed our roles. We knew the leader and his family were under survailence—we had to play up the married part both in public and private. I knew it was a job, but Fiona had never done an undercover mission before. She became too attached to myself and the girl."

"What happened?"

"One of the rebel groups infiltrated the grounds and attempted to kidnap the girl. Fiona and I were able to save her, but there were injuries."

"What kind of injuries?" I sit straighter in my chair.

He sighs. "The girl sustained a gunshot to the shoulder and almost bled out. Fiona lost it. She kept crying about losing her family. I had to pry the girl from her arms so the doctors could save her. The rebel groups were eliminated and the girl made a full recovery, but Fiona didn't. After we got home, she kept calling me or showing up at the offices claiming to be my wife. She emailed me real estate listings for homes in Virginia. It was scary. She lost touch with reality. I finally had to file a formal restraining order and Walt had to speak to her supervisor in the CIA to have her transfered out of the US."

I stare at him for a minute. "Wow. How did she know you were here?"

"I think I can answer that." Walter is in the doorway. He looks between me and Cole. "You straighten out this mess?"

He is talking to Cole, but I answer anyway. "We're good."

Cole's eyes snap to mine, relief washes over his features.

Walter scrubs his neck. "Good." He points to me. "You need to call Abby when we're done here. That girl just verbally kicked my ass." He smiles, looking away. "Love that fiesty kid." His eyes focus back on mine. "I'm a pissed at you, though."

I frown. "You're pissed at me? Why?"

"You thought I'd decieve you and the family? That sucks, Gina."

He's right. I feel terrible. I walk to Walter, wrap my arms around his waist, and bury my head in his chest. "I'm sorry, Walter. I love Cole and hearing he was married threw me so far off course, I was too upset to be rational. I didn't mean to sic Abby on you."

He laughs and strokes my back. "It's fine, Bella."

Him using my nickname means all is forgiven.

Cole clears his throat. "I'm happy you two are all lovey dovey again, but can you please get you hands off my woman and explain how Fiona found me today?"

Walter squeezes me and holds on for another few seconds until we hear Cole make a noise somewhere between a grunt and a growl. Chuckling, Walter lets me go and sits behind my desk. I tried to sit in the chair next to Cole, but he pulls me into his lap with a satisfied grunt. Walter shakes his head, grinning.

"Fiona was sleeping with one of the security guards. That's how she knew about your arrival."

Cole stiffens. "I thought she was in Switzerland?"

Walter nods. "She was, but the company she works for moved it's headquarters here. She moved with them last month. The company was one of the contacts I used to secure an arms deal a few years ago. She had access to some information she shouldn't have; the rest she got from the guard she was sleeping with."

"Shit." Cole's hands tighten on my waist. "She's not going to go quietly, Walt. I need to keep Gina safe. Maybe she should go back to Pennsylvania until this is over."

Walter shakes his head. "I'm not sure that'll help."

I'm pissed. "Hey! You two do realize I'm in the room, right? You don't get to decide my life for me. I'm not leaving."

Cole sighs. "Baby—"

I stand, planting my fists on my hips and squaring off against the two men in the room. “Perhaps I didn’t make myself clear. I’m. Not. Leaving. Now get out of my office. Go figure out what we need to do about psycho bitch. I’ll call Abby before she’s half way across the ocean.”

The men stare at me, but neither make a move.

“Go, gentlemen. Now would be good.”

Walter stands, mumbling something about fiesty, pigheaded women being a pain in his ass as he walks out.

Cole stands and kisses me. “You know that sassy mouth of yours turns me the fuck on, don’t you?”

“Later. Go work with Walter.” I swat his ass, giggling when he spins around his, mouth open. “I think working here will be fun.”

I pick up the phone as Cole chuckles heading for the door. “Hi Abby? It’s fine. There’s no need to have him killed just yet.”

Cole looks over his shoulder at me and winks. I blow him a kiss and calm my cousin.

COLE

The next few weeks are quiet. Gina learns the office programs quickly and makes a few improvements in the filing system.

Everyone loves her. She is quite popular within the office. The women I don't care about, but the male attention doesn't thrill me.

This morning Gina makes Nigel stop at the Starbucks down the street from the office. She gives me a peck on the cheek before hopping out. “Be right back.”

A few minutes later, she comes out with a small box with at least a dozen cups in it. She hands the box to me as she slips into the car. This is our normal Friday routine.

Quickly scanning the box, there are the names of several employees, even Nigel gets a cup.

“Gina, what the hell?”

She shrugs, handing the cup to Nigel. “What? It’s a nice gesture, Cole.”

“Everyone already loves you. No need to make it worse,” I grumble.

She giggles and hands me a cup with my name on it. “Stop it. Drink this. Maybe you’ll be less of a grouch.”

Nigel snickers and I glare at him. He gives me a smirk, raising his cup to his lips. Nigel isn’t such a bad guy. After I found out he is happily married and has six children, I'm not as worried about his interactions with Gina.

We pull up to the office. Nigel hops out of the car to grab the box from Gina while extending a hand to help her out of the car.

“Thank you, Nigel.”

“Thank you for the tea, ma’am. Have a lovely day.” He hands her back the box.

"You, too. See you at six."

Nigel tips his hat to me as he slides behind the wheel. Gina is already through the revolving doors and giving cups to the front desk security guards when I catch up to her.

"Good morning, Bruce, Howard." Each nod before thanking Gina for their beverages.

This is how the first part of the morning goes. Gina drops off cups to people and inquires about their lives. She knows more about these people than Walt and I do, even with the extensive background checks we did on each employee.

Gina's sweet disposition makes everyone open up to her. She is a good listener, compassionate, and kind. My heart swells as each person thanks her for her generosity. Our last stop is to a frail woman in the accounting department. She smiles as Gina approaches her, gratefully accepted the cup. There is a peppermint tea tag hanging out of side.

“Patty, how are you doing today?” Gina sits and holds Patty’s hand.

“Not bad today. Yesterday was bad. I needed to stay home with him. The nurse is there today so I feel better about leaving.”

Gina nods. “I wanted to give you something.” She reaches into her purse, pulling out an envelope. “Use this for him.”

Patty looks in the envelope and gasps. “Miss Toriello, I couldn’t possibly—” She tries to give the envelope back to Gina.

“It’s Gina and yes you can. You use that for whatever he may need and if you need anything else you come let me know.”

A tear rolls down Patty’s cheek. “Thank you,” she whispers. She lookes up. “Oh, Mr. Taylor! My apologies.”

I shake my head. “No worries, Patty. I’m just here to hold the box.”

She blushes. Gina embraces her. "Let's do lunch today, okay? My treat."

Patty simply nods and wipes away another tear.

"What was that about," I ask once we are in the elevator.

"With Patty? Her son is sick."

"Oh. What's he got? The flu?"

Her shoulders slump a little. "No. Her son is seven years old and he's battling Acute Lymphoblastic Leukemia. It's tough for Patty because she's a single mom. Jeremy, her son, has Down's syndrome."

"Jesus."

"Yeah, it's been tough for her. When her boyfriend found out the baby had Down's, he tried to convince Patty to have an abortion, but she refused so he left. He's never seen Jeremy and has never sent her a penny for him, either."

We get off the elevator and head to my office.

"Bastard. I can have him killed for her."

Gina giggles. “Lovely idea, but I already offered and she said no.”

I grin. “You already offered, huh?”

She shrugs. “I’m Italian. When someone we care about is hurting, our first reaction is usually death.”

I sweep her in my arms when we reach the office. “Such violence, Miss Toriello.” I kiss her and take a seat at my desk. “What was in the envelope?”

She walks out of my office, but stops at my question. “Envelope?”

“Gina.” My tone hardens.

She sighs, turning to face me. “It was a check, alright? Patty had to hire a special nurse who could deal with all of Jeremy’s conditions and it’s draining her savings. So I gave her a check to cover Jeremy’s nursing services for the next six months.”

“All of our employees have excellent health insurance, Gina.”

"We do, but a private nurse isn't covered by insurance. Patty has to pay out of pocket."

"Where did you get that kind of money?" I am proud of her, but pissed she didn't tell me about this. I would have handled it.

"Cole, it's no big deal. I got an inheritance when my Nonna died. My parents put it into bonds for me. They matured last year. I rolled the money into my bank account for a rainy day. Patty's dealing with a freaking monsoon. I saw an opportunity to help and took it. End of discussion."

She stands in my office challenging me to question her. Damn if it doesn't make me hard. "End of discussion? Really?"

She juts her chin and plants her hands on her hips. "Yup." When she pops the 'p' at the end, my dick jumps in my slacks.

"Come here."

She glares at me for a brief moment before walking over. She stands in front of my desk. I shake my head. “No, Gina. Stand in front of me.” She comes around the desk, her eyes never leaving mine. “Sit on the desk.”

She moves in front of me and pushes the computer keyboard to the side. Placing her bottom on the edge, she scoots back a few inches. Seductively, Gina crosses her legs. Her skirt slides up her thighs, revealing the black lace silk stocking and garter belt.

Gina started wearing pencil skirts and garters every day, knowing how much I love them. It is sexy, sweet torture for me to see her prance around the office, knowing she is wearing those things to make me happy.

“Baby, you’re the sweetest, most generous woman I have ever met and I love you deeply, but you can’t just give people your money. You should have come to me. I would have handled it.” My hands travel up her calves. She uncrosses her legs.

“Cole, shut up and kiss me.” She pulls me toward her by my tie and claims my mouth. I groan when she slides onto my lap, straddling me. Her skirt hikes up her thighs, revealing the lace tops of her stockings.

“We’re not done discussing this, Gina.” I shift as she grinds deeper into my lap.

“Whatever you say, Mr. Taylor.”

A second later, I pick her up and spin her around. “Put your hands on the desk, Miss Toriello.”

She does as I ask and widens her stance. “Like this, Mr. Taylor?” She glances over her shoulder and smirks.

“Oh, so you want to be cheeky, do you?” I hike her skirt up around her waist, ripping off the scrap of silk she calls underwear, placing it in my pocket.

“Hey! I liked those.”

I gaze at the beauty spread out before me. Gina is so sexy—bare and wanton with just the black lace garter and silk stockings on. My gaze travels down to the black heels she wears, my dick jumps again.

“Gina, I’m going to fuck you bent over my desk with those heels on, but first . . . .”

I draw my hand back and smack her ass.

Gina jumps. “Cole what the hell?”

I rub the place I smacked. Gina relaxes. “That was for being cheeky with me. And this” —I smack the other cheek and then immediately rub the spot— "is for not coming to me with Patty’s problem. We’re a team Gina. That means we work together when someone’s in trouble. Do you understand me?”

When she doesn't answer, I smack her again. “Do you understand?”

Gina moans, pushing back into my hand. “Yes, Cole. I understand.”

“Good girl. Now hold on.” I loosen my belt, unzip; my trousers fall, pooling at my ankles. I shove down my boxers and fuck Gina until she screams my name.

GINA

I squirm in my seat at the thought of this morning's sex in Cole's office. That man can do things most women only read or dream about. I am one lucky bitch. Glancing at my watch, I smirk while picking up the phone. I feel smug and want to rub it in a little.

"Mio Angelo's, how can I help you?"

"Marco! How are you, handsome?"

"Gina! I miss you. When are you going to be done playing sexy security girl and come home?"

My heart thumps a little. It is almost Thanksgiving. It will be my first holiday away from my family. "I like it here, Marco. Why don't you and James come and visit? We could go do the whole tourist thing and shop, go to clubs, out to eat, shop."

"You said shop twice, baby girl."

I giggle. “Yeah, but you know it’s our favorite pastime!”

“True. Alright, alright! Hang on; Abby’s threatening me with a cleaver. Here.”

There is some shuffling, then Abby’s voice. “Hey. Everything alright?”

Marco shouts in the background, “Of course it’s alright. She’s fucking a hot security guy in freaking London for God’s sake!”

I giggle. “Actually, I did that just a few hours ago in the office.”

Abby chuckles. “You slut!”

“That’s my girl,” Marco shouts.

I laugh. “You might as well put me on speaker. Marco’s screaming is distracting me.”

A few minutes later, I say goodbye to my best friends and promise to Skype with Abby later in the week.

Cole comes into my office as soon as I hang up. “Hey, beautiful.”

I smile, crossing to him. "Hey, handsome." I kiss him. "What's up?"

"I'm heading to the gym for a quick workout, but have a surprise for you when you get home."

"Really? What is it?" I wind my arms around Cole's neck, feeling him harden. "Oh, is that it?"

He snickers. "No. It's just my normal reaction to you."

Every time he says something like that, my heart soars. No one has ever made me feel so loved.

"What time will you be home?" Cole nuzzles my neck.

"Around six?"

He nibbles my earlobe. "Perfect." "Bye, gorgeous."

I sigh, watching his fine ass walk out.

A few hours later, I walk into our flat and am greeted with the smells of rosemary chicken. I kick off my heels at the door and creep into the flat. I want to surprise

Cole, but stop dead in my tracks when I hear a woman's voice.

"I mean really, Cole. I've been very patient while you carried on with that whore, but enough is enough."

I peek into the kitchen and almost cry. Cole is unconscious; he is tied to one of the kitchen chairs and gagged with a kitchen towel. There I was a large purple knot over his left eyebrow. Fiona stands at the stove stirring something. She doesn't know I am there.

"My parents were wondering why my husband hasn't been around for a while, but that's all different now."

I watch Cole. His chest rises and falls, but I need him to wake up. Fiona turns from the stove and looks at Cole, she is scowling.

"Cole, are you even listening to me?" She takes a glass with cold water, throwing it at his face. Cole sputters, his eyes fluttering open.

"Ah, there you are husband." Fiona puts the glass in the sink before stalking over to Cole. "Now I'll take this out of your mouth so we can talk, but if you scream or insult me then . . ." She picks up a boning knife off the table in front of Cole. "Our talk will take a different direction. Do you understand?"

Cole nods. Fiona wiggles the gag out of his mouth. "Fiona. How did you get here? Where's Gina?"

"Gina?" Fiona shrieks. "I'm your wife, damn it! Don't you dare utter that whore's name in my presence ever again." She picks up the knife, waving it dangerously close to Cole's cheek. "Understand?"

Cole nods. "I'm sorry, Fiona. Forgive me?"

She placed the knife down then smooths her hands down her jeans. "I don't know why you feel the need to test me, Cole. Aren't I a good wife?"

Cole spots me. Placing my finger in front of my lips, I signal him to keep her talking, creeping backwards.

"Yes, Fiona. You're an excellent wife."

I silently creep to the bedroom, retrieving my Sig Saur from the nightstand drawer. Walter was able to get my guns to our flat without having to go through customs. I check the magazine and chamber a round.

When I creep back to the kitchen, I almost throw up. Fiona had straddled Cole's lap. She is kissing him. Cole's fists are clenched, his knuckles are white; his back ramrod straight. He is not enjoying this.

Fiona ends the kiss and smiles at Cole. "See? Aren't I much better at making you happy than that whore?"

I plant my feet, raising my gun. "You need to stop calling me a whore, you psycho."

Fiona's head snaps to the sound of my voice. "You! Get out of my house!"

I laugh. "It's my house, you crazy bitch, and Cole is mine." I click off the safety.

Fiona jumps off Cole's lap. In one fluid movement, she stands behind him with the knife against his throat.

"If I can't have him, no one can!" The wild look in her eyes scares me for a second.

Cole speaks, “Fiona, please don’t do this to us. You’re right. I was just passing the time with Gina until you came back to me.” He looks at me. I understand what he is doing. “She means nothing to me, Fiona. Nothing.”

Fiona takes the knife away from Cole’s throat. I almost cry in relief. “Do you mean that, Cole?”

He nods. “I do.”

Fiona stands and points the knife at me. “See? He loves me. You lose, whore!”

I pull the trigger. Fiona’s eyes widen. She staggers back and hits the wall. Red blossoms on her blouse above her heart. She slides down the wall, life draining from her eyes.

I stands over her. “I told you not to call me a whore.”

EPILOGUE

"I'm just sorry you're not going to be home for Christmas, Gina. Especially since you missed Thanksgiving."

I am on my cell talking to my mother. "I know, Mom. I miss you guys like crazy, too. Maybe we can come home for Easter?"

"Easter? Vince did you hear that? Gina says maybe she and Cole will come home for Easter! That's four months away. You talk to her!"

"Hey, Bella."

I giggle. "Hi, Dad. Is she losing her mind?"

"Uh-huh."

"Okay, we're walking up the block now. We'll be there in a few minutes."

Dad pretends to give me crap about not coming home for Christmas. “Gina, Easter is too far away. Your mother and I miss you and want to see you before then.”

“That’s right! Just because you’re across an ocean, doesn’t mean I won’t get on a plane and come over there and teach you some damn respect.” Mom is on a rant.

“Ava! Cursing at Christmas?” Dad chuckles. The doorbell rings. “Ava, can you get that? I’m talking to Cole.”

Mom stomps to the door. She throws it open. She is mad as hell. “What—Gina?”

“Hi, Mom.” I pocket my phone. “Merry Christmas.”

She spins and points at my father, narrowing her eyes. “You will pay dearly for this!”

Cole and I come in quickly, hugging mom. “Go easy on him, Mom. He paid for our tickets. We’re your Christmas gift.”

Mom softens and starts to cry. “Damn it, that man still has a way of making me fall in love with him more and more every day!”

That Christmas with my family is the first of many with Cole by my side. He surprises me and everyone by proposing in church after midnight mass on Christmas Eve. Dad and Uncle Ray gave Cole their blessings earlier that day. I am touched that Cole asked them first. I am even more surprised when he gives me the ring. It isn’t a traditional diamond. Cole says after everything we have gone through over the last year, he wants something which represents us. He chose a two carat aquamarine as the center stone and surrounded it with rubies and garnets on a platinum band.

Cole explains the aquamarine represents courage, the garnets represent loyalty, and the rubies represent strength. All the qualities Cole say represent our relationship.

Christmas Day is spent at my parent's house. All the women gather in the kitchen and cook while the men smoke cigars on the porch. I surprise everyone by making the cranberry sauce from scratch. Abby even asks for the recipe. I know she won't use it, but am secretly thrilled that she likes it.

I look across my parent's dining room table at Cole and smile. After Nick died, I thought for sure I will be alone forever, that I am not worthy of love.

Cole smiles back, giving me a flirty wink. I am so grateful he is able to rebuild my love.

ACKNOWLEDGEMENTS

I would like to thank all of my friends and family for their continued support.

Most of all I'd like to thank: Dane, Angelina, Alison, Maggie and Renee Murphy, my kick ass editor!

And of course – a special thank you to you the reader!

I hope you enjoyed Gina's story. Please leave a review on Amazon and Goodreads.

Stay tuned for the next book in the My Love series; Rescue My Love.

Made in the USA
Middletown, DE
31 January 2018